TALES FROM EERIE COUNTY

TABLOID TABBY
BOOK 1

THE HUNCHBACK OF EERIE COUNTY HIGH SCHOOL

TERRY JAMES

PublishAmerica
Baltimore

© 2013 by Terry James.
All rights reserved. No part of this book may be reproduced, stored in a retrieval system or transmitted in any form or by any means without the prior written permission of the publishers, except by a reviewer who may quote brief passages in a review to be printed in a newspaper, magazine or journal.

First printing

All characters in this book are fictitious, and any resemblance to real persons, living or dead, is coincidental.

PublishAmerica has allowed this work to remain exactly as the author intended, verbatim, without editorial input.

Softcover 9781629073828
PUBLISHED BY PUBLISHAMERICA, LLLP
www.publishamerica.com
Baltimore

Printed in the United States of America

For My Father, Terry Sr.
R.I.P.
I Love You!

A HUGE THANKS:

- God.
- My beautiful wife Robin, and my five children: Shelbi, Dallas, Paige, Kailee, and Adalynn for their love and support.
- My mother, My in-laws Gale and Patti S., and Weasel and Connie C., and sister-in-law Sherri C. for words of encouragement throughout the writing process.
- The awesome support and encouragement of my personal Facebook friends. (Too many to list individually, but you know who you are.)
- The awesome crews at Starbucks, (both in Sandusky, Ohio and Toledo, Ohio) for putting up with my hours and hours of pouring over this book and keeping the coffee hot for me.
- My friend Adam Zunk for the awesome help on the cover art.
- Christi and Jeremy M. for proof reading and editing this mess, LOL!
- Jim B., Steve V., Steve L., Steve R., Brian G. and all my other friends at Broadband Express in Toledo and Sandusky for your support as well.
- Jasmine Rodgers for letting me mention her in the book (yes, she is a real person!). For those who have never heard her music, look her up, you will not be disappointed. http://www.jasminerodgers.com

Chapter 1

"Bologna again!" Tabby screamed in a loud, nearly deafening voice from the middle of the cafeteria at Eerie County High School.

It was, of course, the fault of her well-meaning, yet unintentionally evil mother and her diabolical plans to ruin any last surviving trace of sanity left in Tabby's mind.

How could it be a complete coincidence that this moderately discolored mystery meat seemingly finds its way nestled warmly between sheets of slightly stale whole-grain wheat bread? She pondered, *and, as always, smothered in mayonnaise.*

Tabby hated mayonnaise. She hated it a lot. She hated it so much that the mere thought of being within sniffing distance of the white goop would turn her face green and send her digestive system into full reverse. Those closest to her knew, all too well, the sheer terror of Tabby and her "mayo-gag".

On several occasions, she attempted to explain to her mother her dislike for the creamy gunk.

"What are you talking about my dear?" her mother would explain "When, you were little…."

That line seemed to come up a lot in their conversations. Her mother, like many well-meaning parents, seemed to be in complete denial when it came to the fact that their children often grow out of their childhood likes and dislikes. Like the

Wetsy-Betsy Doll she bought her for her fourteenth birthday party.

Inevitably, at the end of each heart-to-heart conversation, her mother would reassure her it would never happen again. But somehow or another, the unwanted delicacy seemed to sneak its way back into her vintage metal lunch box and at 11:45 am each lunch period, Tabby would trade it in for a not-nearly-as-bad-but-still-disgusting peanut butter and margarine sandwich.

The trade-off was of course a survival technique devised and executed with the utmost discretion almost every day between her and Jerry Patterson, the most popular boy in school. Maybe the most popular boy in the whole universe for all anyone knew. He had one of those debonair smiles that could melt even the most cold-hearted ninth grade cheerleader. He dressed like a millionaire, smelled like a cologne factory, and was the key to the unstoppable force behind the Eerie County High School Executioners junior varsity football team.

Tabby, on the other hand, was not exactly the popular, high fashion, social butterfly type. In fact, she strived to be the anti-popular. Her jet-black hair was bowl cut about ear length and was normally tied up in two pony tails fixed to each side of her head. She kept a closet filled with nothing but black and red clothing generally purchased at thrift stores and garage sales. She considered them retro, and wore them out of spite. This was mainly to show the fashion industry who was actually controlling the tide of fashion, or at least in her own small corner of the universe.

As a substitution to the seemingly endless hours of moronic socializing with the rest of the cattle in the school, she took on journalism and wrote regularly in the school newspaper. Her articles mostly consisted of rants and protest pieces, but once in a while a gem would come out of it. She was a great writer, which was a good thing because it was exactly what she wanted to do when she grew up.

For some unforeseen reason though, Jerry had missed the last four days of school, thus leaving Tabby to stare horrifically at the slightly deformed sandwich bag with the nasty puss-like slime plastered inside.

Sitting across from Tabby was her best friend April, who at this point was beginning to slide slightly to the right, out of Tabby's possible projection path. She could always tell long before anyone else when Tabby was going to blow chunks.

April was a quiet girl who spent most of her time with a book in front of her nose, mostly informational and text books. Her style was quite a bit more conservative than that of Tabby's, mostly flower dresses and her favorite white dress shoes. She didn't so much walk as she seemed to float around the school with an innocent smile that made her look much younger than she was.

But, despite April's seemingly gentle and kind exterior, she had the mind of a demented- borderline psychopath which lay just beneath the surface. She really hated cheerleaders. Though, it wasn't so much hatred as it was an outright delusional, malevolent, and antagonistic rage. One whose very origins were locked in an infinite realm of secrecy, so deep in April's psyche that not even she could fully comprehend it. But she didn't have to understand it. She thrived on it.

But, of course, no true friendships ever came in pairs. A third person would arrive shortly who more or less kind of glued the trio together. He was what the other two considered the go to guy when it came to settling disputes, or getting them out of trouble.

Thomas had always been a rather level headed fellow who seemed to have an answer for everything. He'd always thought of his friendship with the other two to be a happy coincidence. Even though he usually found himself getting the short end of the stick when it came to doing Tabby and April's dirty work, and cleaning up afterwards sometimes as well.

He wasn't much to look at when it came to personal appeal. He was slightly, but not noticeably overweight. His choice of attire was conservative, not at all flashy like many boys his age. His light brunette and blondish hair, though somewhat groomed, still seemed to display a subtle hint of un-refinement.

"Didn't make it to school again today, huh?" Thomas asked as he approached the table just behind Tabby.

April stared at Thomas with a blank look on her face. "What do you think genius?" she replied.

He looked down cautiously in Tabby's direction and began to notice the ever more greenish color in her face. Without further hesitation, he quickly scooped up the menacing sandwich and tossed it into a nearby garbage can.

"Come on dear," Thomas sighed, "guess I can buy you something in the cafeteria."

"I thought you were trying to keep me from gagging?" said Tabby as she stood up from her chair and quickly scanned the immediate area for a hint of the latest lunchroom concoction. Meatloaf, mashed potatoes, green beans, and the famous carton of milk with the picture of some poor missing soul printed on it, the same picture that has been printed on them since they started preschool. She imagined Jerry's face printed on the side for a quick moment before snapping back to reality.

"I wonder why he hasn't been here. Do you think he's sick or something?" asked Tabby as they walked slowly to the back of the steadily growing lunch line.

Thomas sighed again. He seemed to be doing that a lot this week. "I don't know, for one. I really don't care for two, and for three, why don't you just go to his house and ask him yourself?"

"What!" Tabby answered in a nearly ear-splitting voice, and then noticed their conversation was getting loud and began to whisper, "What? You mean actually go to his house? What if someone sees me? They'd think I liked him or something. Not to mention if Carrie Guile saw me, they've been dating for like, ever now. She'd beat me down and then some."

"Well, you do like him right?" asked Thomas with a quirky grin on his face.

"Heck no, don't even go there!" she answered loudly, and then noticed that her voice had gotten out of control again, and reset her volume to a personal level yet again, "Why would you say that?"

"I'm just joking!" said Thomas, "Besides the whole school already knows they broke up last week. Of course if you bothered to talk to people you'd-"

"They broke up!" Tabby interrupted, once again way too loud, this time she noticed people starting to stare. "When did you plan on telling me this? What if he moved away?"

"Then I would ask you to get a job to start paying for your own lunches," answered Thomas with his usual sheepish grin. "You're killing my wallet this week. More than usual."

Tabby smiled understandingly, she had been relying a lot on him lately to keep her nourished during the day. It's not that she didn't appreciate the kind gesture, but the fact that she was somehow worried so much about Jerry that she hadn't noticed that she had been sort of taking advantage of him. Besides, it wasn't like she really cared about Jerry that much anyways. If anything, it was more of a curiosity about why he was not in school. "You know I wuv ya right?" she asked as she grabbed a tray off the shelf, discolored and stained with the unmentionable cuisines of years past.

"Yes my wuv," Thomas smiled back.

"So you want me to go with you to his house later to check on him. I could even help you write a love letter for him as well if you like?" Thomas laughed as he began to prepare for the elbow nudge that was sure to come.

Tabby quickly, but softly, elbowed him in the ribs. He had a habit of picking on her when it came to Jerry. But the fact of the matter remained. He was missing from school, and Tabby was going to get to the bottom of it. *But first*, she thought to herself with a disgusted grimace on her face, *let's try to survive lunch.*

A dark and loathsome figure hunched quivering in the back of an unlit closet on the second floor at 123 West Guillotine Row. It nervously rocked back and forth on its knees as it applied what had to be the hundredth layer of cologne since it woke up that morning. It had been this way for the last few mornings.

"What the heck happened to me?" it continuously thought to itself as it stared dreadfully at a small handheld mirror that it had not let go of for at least four days. In the midst of its long and deep thoughts, it had already eliminated several possibilities for his condition. acne, puberty, allergic reaction to cologne, food poisoning though it was still a possibility the way his mom cooks, and last but not least, leprosy.

Suddenly, there was a knock on the door. No doubt it was its mother again.

"Honey? You have been in that room now for four days straight. You either come out of there or I'm busting down the door!" its mom called, slightly muffled from the other side of the door.

This is bad, It thought to itself as it unscrambled its thoughts to find yet another reason to keep anyone outside the room.

"I'll be down in a little bit!" it cried out, sticking its head slightly out of the closet door. "I'm feeling a little better, but I want to make sure so I don't get anyone else sick." To add an element of realism to the "sick" excuse it had been playing out till now, it added a few fake yet realistic sounding coughs.

"OK, Baby," its mother replied in a relieved and mildly satisfied voice. "But I expect you to get out of that bed sometime today, I made another appointment with the doctor and this time you're going."

Somehow it doubted that the doctor could help him, except putting it in the freak show at the carnival. It thought to itself as it stared yet again at itself in the mirror. *Now how am I going to get myself out of this one?*

It softly began to cry.

CHAPTER 2

The trip home from school each afternoon was a madhouse aboard bus number 13. The seating arrangement from previous generations of students had pretty much stayed the same.

Starting from the back, you had the sports junkies, who spent the ride home making as much noise as possible. Yelling, extreme laughter, wadded up paper bouncing off the back of other people's heads, footballs being caught, basketballs being bounced off the backs of seats, and the indistinguishable chatter of last week's sporting events thundered from the back almost daily.

Seated prominently in front of them were the ever famous, ever popular, Eerie County High School cheerleading squad, April's least favorite spot which she sometimes got stuck inhabiting. From here, the seemingly endless chatter over the latest gossip could be heard, not to mention the almost daily poll of which jock had the cutest butt. Their pointless and mindless conversations resounded nearly as loudly as that of the previous section.

Just ahead of them lay the masses of students whose status and class were widely considered undeterminable. They neither shared the prestige of upper social class status nor wallowed in the fermented, rank depths of the socially rejected. This tended to be the quieter section of the bus, though you could barely tell from the calamity behind them.

Then there was the front of the bus, the section predestined by all as the "loser's section". The socially scorned, nerds, heavy metal freaks, emos, nose pickers, and pizza faces. This was also the location of what was considered the worst seat on the bus, which was the seat directly behind the bus driver, who generally looked like he was ready to strangle someone and smelled like a burning ashtray doused in hard liquor.

Of course this is exactly where you would find Tabby seated voluntarily. She would sit right next to the window, with her knees pulled up to her chin reading or talking with Thomas or April, whichever one ended up climbing into the bus first, usually April.

But on Thursdays, no one talked to Tabby. It was because Thursday was the day her favorite weekly tabloid newspaper came out, and she was always way too captivated to carry on any type of reasonable conversation.

The paper, The Eerie Truth Weekly, started its circulation about midway through Tabby's eighth grade year of school. It was written, edited, illustrated, and printed locally by a man named Glimpin Dimbwick. That name alone was enough to know just how silly the articles in the paper sounded.

Articles in the paper ranged from dogs with bat wings, living dead corpses in a hidden cemetery near Butcher Lake, aliens having secret meetings with city council members over proposed interstellar dumping permits, and the dumbest one of all, a walking hand drawn stick figure named Sketchy who just leapt off the pages of some poor unsuspecting third grader's construction paper and disappeared late last year.

She believed absolutely nothing that was printed in the thing, but for her, it was the best form of entertainment this area had to provide. She kept every issue like a collector's item, read it carefully from cover to cover, and then slipped it into a plastic sleeve to help preserve it. It was modern journalism at its worst, but it was highly imaginative. Thomas and April didn't get why she was so interested, but knew Tabby well enough to keep to themselves when she was reading.

"This week's top story" Tabby read enthusiastically as she began flipping to the first page, "Demon from Hell Found Dead near hidden Cemetery, Corpses Liberated!"

Not this story again! Tabby thought to herself. *This guy really needs some new material.*

"You know, I would have never believed it had I not seen it with my own eyes." Thomas said as he boarded the bus just in time for the doors to shut. "Did you notice that Lisa Hamler and Adam Deshler are sitting together? And even holding hands, who'd have thought?"

"And I care why?" Tabby asked softly with a hint of irritability in her voice for the uninvited interruption.

"Come on," Thomas answered "You're not even a little interested in the fact that a high school cheerleader is now dating a borderline nerd herd member?"

"Good for them, and no not really," Tabby replied, never taking her eyes off the paper.

Thomas sat quietly next to her, glimpsing over from time to time to see what she was reading. He had brought his music player to school so he had something to listen to on the way home, besides the sound of Tabby reading quietly to herself, which normally involved giggling and rereading aloud to whomever was sitting next to her. Usually it was April, but for some reason, she stayed behind at school. She had told Thomas something about superglue, a pair of scissors, and the cheerleading squad's pom-poms.

"It is best not to ask too many questions." April explained earlier that afternoon, "Knowledge is not only power, it could also make you an accessory."

Thomas's taste in music was quite similar to Tabby's. He quite often steered away from the more popular hit music and instead preferred more independent artist. It was one of the dozens of things he shared in common with Tabby which more often than not made people believe they were a couple, though it couldn't be any further from the truth. It's not that it couldn't happen, but both had found that it would just get in the way of the happy place they had already resided in, at least Tabby thought of it that way.

After about fifteen minutes or so, Thomas decided it was time to break the bubble of silence again, "So, anything interesting in this week's commode companion?"

"Not really," answered Tabby. "But the half boy/half porcupine twins were finally adopted by the Bard Family, they should be proud."

Thomas laughed. "How can you read this junk? It gets worse and worse with every issue. Just look at this article Hunchback Spotted Climbing Face of Local High School, you'd think something like that would have been all over the regular news?"

"That's because the regular news agencies lack the creative journalism found in the lower, misunderstood tabloid newspaper world. They're constant search for true life sensationalism blinds them to the real picture of exactly what didn't happen," Answered Tabby sarcastically. "It takes a true artist to paint a verbal picture of untruth and make believe."

"Yea, but don't you think writing a story involving a made up literary creature and our high school, slash prison, is a little close to home? I mean, who would want to break into that place?" asked Thomas.

"I'm not sure, but it does make for a strange coincidence that there would be a mysterious figure roaming around the school at all hours on the night before Jerry stopped coming to school." replied Tabby as she read further into the suspicious article. "He doesn't list any names of witnesses either. So who would have reported it?"

"Why do you care?" Thomas asked. "All this junk is made up anyways, no one reported it."

"I know it's made up. But you would think that the writer would have listed witnesses to substantiate the claims even if it were made up."

"So, do you think your beloved has anything to do with this do you?" Thomas asked with his usual quirky smile he sports when he begins to tease her about the imaginary love affair.

"No, he doesn't look anything like a...." she paused for a moment as she analyzed what was just said.

"HE IS NOT MY BELOVED!" she yelled, then noticed that people were staring at her. She quickly followed up with a quick jab to his side with her elbow then continued with what she was saying.

"How could anyone mistake him for a hunchback? The guy is tall and thin, not short and lumpy. Besides, you could smell him a mile away, anybody could pick him from a lineup," She explained, this time with a slight hint of irritation in her voice.

Thomas rubbed his side. He foolishly did not expect the jab and was now half desperate to change the subject. "So is there anything in there about a man who finds his soul mate in a small guppy?"

Tabby turned slowly from the pages she had till then been so fixated on and looked Thomas right in the eyes, "It wasn't a guppy. It was a beta."

"Come on!" Thomas replied loudly, "You have to be kidding?"

"Yes I am, so stop making fun of my choice of extracurricular reading material. You don't see me saying anything about your girly manga magazines."

"My manga is not girly," returned Thomas, as the school bus began to stop at Tabby's usual drop off. "Just because it's a romance about a blood thirsty half-demon and an unsuspecting teenage girl in futuristic Neo-Tokyo, does not make it a girly manga mag."

"Just meet me at the corner of Bog and Guillotine at four," Tabby said as she stood up and began to shove her way past an unmoving Thomas. "And no more funny business about me and Jerry, it ain't going to happen."

"Ain't isn't a real word," Thomas joked again as she finished pushing past him.

"Yes it is," Tabby shot him a sideways glance as she approached the bus door which was beginning to open. "Four pm today, please."

Why he never told her no, he could never figure out. "Sure, don't worry I'll be there," Thomas answered still rubbing his side as he considered how he could fit a small pillow to keep in his shirt for times like these. "Me and my ice pack wouldn't miss this for the world."

Four o'clock rolled around quickly. Of course Tabby's mother had a small list of chores to be completed which Tabby nearly always neglected. Tabby wasn't exactly lazy, but when one kept their bedroom immaculate every minute of the day, cleaning it seemed to be a waste of time.

At 3:59, Tabby arrived at the meeting spot. Thomas arrived shortly after and they began to make their way down the road. About half way down the block or so, April appeared out of nowhere looking slightly panicked, but in a confident way.

"Did anyone follow you?" Tabby asked April jokingly as she quickly glanced around.

April answered quietly, "No, I think I got out just in time before they arrived to start practice. By the way, do cheerleaders wear hats when they practice?"

"I'm not sure, probably not. Why do you ask?" answered Thomas.

"Good," April said. "And don't ask, I'm sure you'll hear about it tomorrow."

Thomas looked at April with a hint of dread in his face. "I'm not sure I want to. By the way, you have some glitter on your face."

"Damn, evidence!" April whispered loudly. "I need to get cleaned up. Umm, whatever you two are doing, just pretend I'm there making smart comments and getting into things I shouldn't. I'll catch up later."

Then as quickly as she arrived, she disappeared, leaving Thomas and Tabby to wonder what she was up to. Both looked at each other then proceeded down the road to Jerry's house. Not that they had far to go, before they knew it, they were standing at the front door.

"Well, knock," Thomas said as he watched Tabby stare at the door for several moments. "You know, you knock on the door with your knuckles. Then someone comes to the door from the inside and opens it up."

"I know how to knock dummy," replied Tabby quietly. "I'm just thinking maybe this was not a good idea and-"

Just then the front door opened and Tabby's heart about jumped out of her chest. Then it began to slow down when they saw it was just Jerry's mother.

"Tabby Grimshaw, is that you?" asked Jerry's mother as she stared at her with one of those nostalgic looks that most mothers are good at.

In truth, Jerry and Tabby were really good friends up until the sixth grade. They used to play together nearly every day after school, they were quite inseparable. But as most childhood friendships go, as junior high starts, old friendships end, and new ones begin. Jerry quickly climbed the ropes of popularity, and Tabby chose to neglect the status quo and concentrate on school and writing.

"In the flesh," Tabby answered, conjuring the brightest smile she could. "Is Jerry here by any chance? We haven't seen him at school all week."

"Oh dear, my poor baby has been cooped up in his room for days. I can't get him to come out for nothing," answered Jerry's mom with a look of concern plastered on her face. Then she leaned forward just a little towards Tabby. "May I say you have grown up so much since I'd seen you last, and grown so beautifully. Why don't you two hang out anymore?"

"I'm not sure really," Tabby answered back with a slight hint of a blush on her cheeks. Tabby really didn't consider herself much to look at, and was often taken aback when she was complimented. "Well, I guess let him know we stopped by and-"

"Perhaps we can go upstairs and try and coax him out of his room?" interrupted Thomas as he shot Tabby a look and whispered. "You can elbow me later for this."

Jerry's mother considered the proposal for a moment. "That sounds like a wonderful idea!" She began to open the door all the way to let them in. "Maybe a little company from an old friend will cheer him up."

Tabby shot Thomas a very stern look as they began to enter Jerry's house. Well, it was more like Thomas walked in the door pushing Tabby as he did, but not so much that it was extremely noticeable.

"Do you remember which room it is dear?" as the two approached the steps.

"Yes," answered Tabby. "Second room to the right, right?"

Thomas and Tabby began to climb the stairs, they both heard a slight rustling from the back of the hall. "Come on, there's no turning back now," Thomas said with a smile on his face. Tabby knew in her gut that he was enjoying this way too much.

The door to Jerry's bedroom was typical of most high school boys. A poster of a girl in a bikini that was obviously doctored, another poster of a prominent football hero bound to have his career ended early on some scandal, and the ever popular "KEEP OUT" sign. Tabby had one herself though it never seemed to work. She looked for the exposed portion of the door and began to knock.

"Anyone home in there?" Tabby announced in as clear and as quiet a voice as she could muster. "It's Tabby and Thomas."

There was a long silence, several long silences to be exact, "Well I guess he's sleeping. Guess we should go?" said Tabby as she began to turn only to be stopped by Thomas.

Thomas pounded on the door hard, "Hey!" he shouted, "You awake in there?"

Several more seconds went by followed by more rustling from behind the door, much louder than before. The two looked at each other for yet another moment then turned back to the door.

"We're not leaving until you answer!" shouted Tabby, now beginning to get a little perturbed over the fact that he was not saying anything. "I swear I will beat down this door, then you!"

"Go away!" A loud voice finally answered from the other side of the door. It sort of sounded like Jerry, but at the same time, didn't.

"Why aren't you coming to the door? You know everyone is worried about you," Thomas answered back.

"I don't care, just leave," said the voice, slightly louder than the first time he spoke.

"He doesn't sound happy to hear us," said Thomas as he turned to Tabby. "Maybe we should go?"

"Hell no!" answered Tabby with an unusual sternness to her voice. "He's not getting out of this one. I am tired of being ignored. We used to be friends, now I'm lucky to get a nod when we trade sandwiches. He is not all high and mighty and he will tell us what is going on!"

Tabby reared her foot and kicked the door with everything thing she had, and the door flew open. She closed her eyes for a moment hoping he was decent then stepped into the room opening one eye cautiously. It was empty.

Tabby quickly scanned the room and there was absolutely no sign of life anywhere. That was until she spotted the closet door slowly creep shut on the far side of the room.

"Please," the voice from inside the closet asked, now quieter and almost sobbing. "Please just leave, I don't want anyone to see me like this."

"Like what?" she asked as she slowly made her way to the closet door. "You know I could care less what you look like. It's not like I haven't seen you with bed head before."

"It's a little more serious than a simple case of a bad hair day," answered the voice from the other side of the closet door. "And what do you mean I don't talk to you? You don't talk to me."

"How can I when you got your head that far up your other friend's butts. Let's face it, when popularity and puberty hit, our friendship was gone. Now I'm back and you're not going anywhere until I know what's going on."

"Why? So you can put it in the school paper. Maybe you'd like to take a few pictures while you're at it."

"Please stop fighting you two," Thomas finally stepped in. "We hadn't seen you in a few days and were just wondering if you were OK. Don't get mad at us for being concerned."

"Well I'm here, I'm fine, now get out," said Jerry. Now Tabby was beginning to boil.

"Just tell us what's wrong," She asked as she kneeled down next to the door. "I promise, no paper, no pictures, I just want to help, as a friend."

"I don't think you can help me with this one Tabby," Jerry said as he finally opened the closet door slowly.

Tabby gasped, "Oh my god!"

What she saw looked nothing like Jerry at all. The figure behind the door was something out of a bad horror movie. He was half bald with his forehead protruding out just past the point of his nose. One of his eyes looked as though it were ready to fall out. His body looked smashed and beaten with a very pronounced hump on his back. One of his legs was prominently thicker than the other and was stubby and crooked. His skin was discolored with a slight tint of yellow and looked rough and hairy. But above all, the usual overwhelming scent of the manliest cologne Jerry could find was replaced by an indescribable stench that nearly put Tabby on the floor.

She couldn't speak. She couldn't do anything for several moments. All she could do stare at him with her mouth open. She felt paralyzed and numb. Then, she managed to utter her first few words, "Did you get hit by a car?"

Thomas was just as equally shocked, maybe more so than Tabby. He also had trouble putting the situation together in his mind. "Maybe a train?"

"No, I didn't get hit by anything," Jerry answered. "Or at least I don't think I was hit by anything."

"Maybe it's an allergic reaction to your cologne?" Tabby added, still unable to stop staring at him.

"I already thought about it, still wearing the same kind since eighth grade." Replied Jerry looking aggravated, or at least the other two guessed that was the look they were looking at.

Jerry shook his head and began to sit down on the closet floor, "I've been trying to figure this out for days, nothing I come up with makes any sense. I went to bed Saturday night looking like me, and woke up Sunday morning looking like Quansa-mata."

"That's Quasimodo, you numb-skull." Tabby corrected him, "Do you even read the books we're assigned in school?"

"I sort of skimmed though it between school and football practice" Jerry answered.

"Well that doesn't make much sense." Thomas replied with a puzzled look on his face. "How does one become the Hunchback of Notre-Dame overnight?"

"I have no idea." Tabby said still staring at Jerry with a look of disbelief.

Then a voice called out from the hallway just outside the door, it was Jerry's mother. "Is everything OK in here?"

Thomas quickly reached over and slammed the door just as Jerry's mother was about to enter the room. "Everything's fine Mrs. Patterson, nothing to worry about." He shrugged and looked at Tabby for some sort of inspiration as to what to say next.

"Um, yea everything's fine, um, we are just talking to him about some homework assignments he has. Wow, you are really falling behind, better get started right away catching up, I will help you with this first part." Tabby belted out as she began to scratch her head on how to deal with the real issue at hand.

"OK," Jerry's mother shouted from the other side of the door. "I'll bring you some snacks."

"No!" All three said completely in unison.

"I think we will be just fine, besides I'm on a diet." she lied, as if her 110 pound frame really needed it.

"Well, OK then." his mom answered back from the other side of the door. All three could hear her footsteps move away from the door and down the staircase.

"That was too close." Tabby said as she sat back on her feet and stared at Jerry with a bewildered look on her face. She had no clue where to start with helping him out with this impromptu disfigurement. Then all at once it hit her like a ton of bricks. "You've been to the school since this happened?"

"Yea, I climbed out my window late Sunday night. I wanted to go to the school to see if I had any cologne there, I was running out here." Jerry explained.

"Really, you left your house in the middle of the night, made your way to the high school, risked your life climbing the face of the school, and broke in illegally so you could layer on more cologne," She commented as she began to reach into the black satchel she quite frequently carried with her.

"What is that supposed to mean?" Jerry shot back, "Besides, it's not like anyone saw me, it was completely dark."

Tabby looked him square in the eye. She was going to have to give it to him straight. "Jerry, you wear way too much cologne." She sighed in relief. "There, I said it. You smell like a cologne factory that is burning down. The reason you win so many football games is because the other team's eyes are watering and can't see the ball. Your poor terrier pooch in the back yard will never make a good hunting dog because you killed it's sense of smell, and not to mention the-"

"OK, you made your point-" Jerry jumped in with a half-hearted attempt to mount a counter strike against Tabby's verbal assault, but was quickly lashed at again.

"Don't interrupt me, I'm on a roll. As I was saying, and not to mention, someone did see you." Tabby pulled out her copy of The Eerie Truth Weekly and handed it to Jerry. "Somebody saw you at the school and now it is all over town."

Jerry stared at the article in complete disbelief. "I...I don't believe it. How could this have happened? I swear I was completely alone. It had to be like three o'clock in the morning. Who the heck would be awake at three o'clock in the morning on a Tuesday?"

"I don't know," answered Tabby with an inquisitive look on her face, "But we are going to find out."

"Um, what do you mean we?" asked Thomas from behind her, standing guard at the door like a nervous convict. "Why would we help him? You don't even like the guy, remember?"

"It doesn't matter how I feel about this lug-head, I was always taught that we should always bear the burdens of others, no matter how we feel." Tabby paused for a moment to look at Jerry. She really could have cared less to let him face his predicament alone, but that darn Sunday school lesson pounded at the back of her mind. "Besides, do you think he's smart enough to do this on his own? He can barely tie his shoes let alone take time to properly research his condition."

Jerry looked up in what seemed to be a look of appreciation. For the first time since they got there and probably for the last four days or so, he smiled.

"I guess." answered Thomas, as he sat back and rolled his eyes. "So miss smarty pants, what is our first move?"

Tabby thought for a moment, "First move, we don't tell April about this."

"Don't tell April bout what?" April's voice suddenly shot out from the other side of the room. It almost scaring the life out of the other three.

Tabby stared in utter disbelief as April stepped out from the back corner with her head leaning to one side and her arms crossed.

"You better not say a word of this to anyone," Tabby said as she stood up to face her directly. "How in the heck did you get in here anyways?"

"Like anyone else who has friends who try to sneak their significantly disfigured, ex-childhood friend behind their back… the window," April answered in an innocent yet mischievous voice. "Don't worry, nobody would believe me anyways. That is if I had anyone to tell anyways. So, can I at least take a picture?"

Thomas shot her a quick look of disbelief.

"What?" April shot back with her own look of disbelief, "Think of it as collateral. You never know when you'll need to-"

"April!" Thomas and Tabby said in unison.

"I'm joking, or am I?" April admitted looking at Jerry. "So where does our little misadventure take us first. I could do a little browsing on the internet to see if anything like this has happened before. Maybe Mr. Quasimodo has a twin somewhere?"

"Good, you do that, and the rest of us are going to take a little visit to a local tabloid newspaper to see if Mr. Glimpin Dimbwick knows what might be going on, and who this mystery witness might be." Tabby added with a hint of excitement in her voice. Her first investigation, not that she could write about it, but it would make for good practice.

Chapter 3

Tabby could not get Jerry's image out of her head. She just couldn't imagine how he must feel right now. She was wondering at the same time why she even cared. There were a lot of questions that needed to be answered. Like how did it happen, who or what was responsible, and how to get him back to normal? But even more so than the questions surrounding Jerry's personal predicament, was the fact that a tabloid newspaper reported it accurately.

If this guy was right about Jerry's midnight romp around the high school, what else in this simple tabloid journalistic junk was real? Tabby thought quietly to herself as she finished folding her cloths and putting them away back at her house.

She stopped for a moment to take a quick glance at the clock. It was 7:10 pm. The gang would be meeting up soon to head over to the local newspaper building, The Eerie County Daily. According to the front cover of The Eerie Truth Weekly, it was printed in this building, but no other address or phone number was listed for the tabloid which seemed really strange. She could only assume that it all happened in the same building, since the tabloid wrote mostly local happenings, then Glimpin Dimbwick had to be local as well. It was a long shot anyways.

But before anything could happen, Tabby had to figure out how to talk her mother into allowing her fifteen-year-old daughter out of the house after 7:30 at night, a formidable feat just by itself. Her mother was pretty protective. It would take an Act of God to talk her into it.

"Hey mom, can I go to Thomas's house tonight to study for our test tomorrow?" she asked as she stood outside her bedroom door. "I promise to come straight home afterwards. My laundry is done, leftovers from dinner are put away, and dishes are done."

"I don't think so dear, it's awfully late," her mother replied.

"Come on! You can't keep treating me like a baby. I'm 16 years old now!" Tabby pleaded to her mother who had just sat down to read a few more chapters of her book.

"You know how I feel about you being out after dark. Besides you had all afternoon to study, maybe you should have done it then," her mother said, not once taking her eyes off the pages she was engrossed in.

"We stopped after school to visit a friend who has been sick from school. We took him his homework. Beside, Thomas only lives a block away, nothing will happen I promise."

Her mother sighed as she put down the book and stared at Tabby with worried eyes. "Well, I guess you're not a little girl anymore. I'll tell you what. I want you home by nine o'clock on the nose,"

Wow she was giving up rather easily. Tabby thought to herself, but in no way was she going to argue the point any further. OK, well maybe a little.

"How about nine-thirty, we got a lot to cover. Thomas can walk me home afterwards?" she asked with a slight glimmer of excitement in her voice.

Her mother sighed again. "Fine, but he better be at that front door when you get here."

"Thanks mom, I love you!" she kissed her mom on the cheek, grabbed her satchel, and headed out the door.

She began to dart as quickly down the road as her legs would carry her. The newspaper building was a good twenty minute walk from her house, and the gang would be there shortly. "I hope Jerry was able to sneak out of his house without being seen, that's all we need is this story making to the real newspaper." she thought to herself.

About half way there she spotted a shadow that appeared to be following her. She began to get nervous. *What if my mom was right? Maybe going out alone was not such a great idea?*

She began to run faster as the shadow seemed to move faster with her. Her heart was pounding out of her chest. She suddenly decided to stop the nonsense, and to investigate the shadow. She stopped abruptly and began to look around. But the mysterious shadow figure seemed to just vanish into thin air.

She stood silent for a moment listening to the cool breeze as it pushed its way through the trees. "Something is not right." She thought to herself as she slowly brushed a few strands of her hair back behind her ear.

She began to turn around when she abruptly smacked into a short hooded figure standing right behind her. She gasped in horror as she backed up a step to see who or what she had run into. In the dark, she had a hard time making out any facial features, but could tell that it was majorly disfigured.

She swallowed hard as she managed barely to utter a single question just under her breath, "Jerry, is that-"

"Why are you helping me, this time for real?" muttered the dark figure as he took a step forward into the light, revealing the tattered facial features that had burned into Tabby's mind just a few hours earlier.

"I...um..." Tabby managed to stumble out of her mouth as she still attempted to get her wits back.

Jerry looked at her in disbelief, "You're not just doing this because of a sandwich. There has to be some other reason. Maybe I'm being roped in for one of your little article pieces in the school paper? Maybe improve your social status amongst your fellow classmates? Or maybe, just maybe, you finally found a way to destroy my reputation?"

"Or maybe you just need a friend instead of a locked closet," she shouted back. "Let's face it, if you truly thought you could depend on those so called friends you have at that school, you'd have been out with them trying to figure this out. But you know as well as I do that without your looks, athletic ability and classy wit, you're nothing in their eyes. Maybe even less than I am."

She looked him square in the face as the stark reality of what she just said landed squarely on his heart. "How many of your so-called friends have stopped and checked on you in the last few days? Does the phrase out of sight, out of mind mean anything to you?"

He sighed to himself as his eyes left hers and drifted slowly to the ground. He realized she was right. His mouth began to open as though to say something, but then closed as though still searching for the right thing to say. Finally after a short moment he looked back up at her, guilty for doubting her.

"I guess I have been a little shallow lately, but I never really wanted to hurt anyone. I got caught up in excitement of being popular. I never really meant to hurt anyone, especially you. I'm sorry for doubting you, any help you can offer, I will gladly accept." Jerry admitted with what looked like a smile of gratitude on his face.

"Let's just get going," she said as she began to rush him down the street, partly to avoid missing the others, partly to escape the awkward moment they created. "We don't have much time, the others are probably waiting."

Within fifteen minutes, Tabby met up with the others and were now standing in front of the newspaper entrance. All except Jerry of course who chose to remain hidden not far away behind a recycle bin just around the other side of the building. They look up at the four-story building which housed not only the newspaper offices, but also other assorted government agencies and private businesses whose building locations were clearly marked on a board outside the double doors. As suspected, <u>The Eerie Truth Weekly</u> was not one of them.

"How are we going to find this guy in this huge building?" Thomas asked as he analyzed the directory for what had to be the fifth or sixth time. "It's not on the directory, maybe he's not here?"

Tabby looked as well hoping he had missed something. "Well, someone inside here has to know something. I guess we will just have to go in and ask."

"Are you kidding?" April asked. "Nobody is going to talk to a bunch of adolescent teenagers. Besides, the sign over there says they're closed. Guess we will have to come back tomorrow?"

"We're getting in tonight!" Tabby answered back as she began to walk towards the door. She needed answers, and she was going to get them. At least she thought that's what a real journalist would do.

The door felt heavy as she pulled it open to reveal the first floor. Just inside there were a set of elevators to the right followed by the main doors into the lobby of the main newspaper. She walked briskly with April and Thomas in tow to the door and peered in. Most of the employees had gone home for the evening, but a few late writers sat typing feverishly at their computers as though racing against some unknown clock to make their deadline.

Tabby was excited to see firsthand what it was like to work at a real newspaper, but just as quickly snapped her brain back to the matter at hand as she began to open the door to the lobby.

"What do you kids want? We're closed!" shouted a guard from inside the door as the three entered.

"We just had a few ques-" Tabby was able to mutter out before the security guard interrupted.

"Did you not hear me? I said we're closed!" shouted the security guard again as he got up from his chair and began to walk around his desk and towards the trio. "This is no place for children."

The guard was about medium height, grossly overweight, shirt half tucked in with nothing more threatening to guard with but an oversized flashlight mounted like a sidearm on a cop. He was slightly elderly looking, and apparently very upset that he had to get up from his nap to deal with the adolescent intruders.

"We're looking for Glimpin Dimbwick!" Tabby shot out hoping to get her point across before she was interrupted again.

"Nobody by that name here," shouted the guard again, "Now, get out before I throw you out on your butt!"

"But it's an emergency, we have to find him!" Thomas shouted back, "Do you know how we can-"

"I SAID OUT!" the guard screamed, moving even faster now and beginning to reach for the flash light.

The trio spun around as fast as they could and darted out the door. As the door slammed behind them, they could hear the door lock being latched and the guard cursing loudly to himself as he hobbled slowly back to his desk. The three took a quick breath then looked at one another in disbelief.

"Man, he needs a few more pots of calm-the-heck down," April uttered, as they peeked back inside to see if he was still watching. The guard was still staring at them as he picked up his copy of some military magazine, and then looked away and continued reading as though nothing had happened.

"He's just grumpy because he has accomplished nothing in his life," an unknown voice answered from behind them.

Slightly confused, they spun around to find a young man standing behind them with a look of secrecy on his face as he glanced around nervously, then turned his attention back to them. The guy looked like he was still in high school, but no one in the group recognized him. He had buck teeth, a thin frame, small wiry glasses, and more freckles than Tabby had ever seen on another human being.

"Who are you?" asked April.

"I'm Simon. I'm an in-school intern down in the mail room here," he replied.

"So how come we've never seen you in the hallways at school?" Tabby asked.

"My mom home schooled me and thought this would be a great place to get my start as a real reporter," he smirked as he looked down his glasses at the three. "So you're looking for the weird guy, huh?"

Tabby stared in disbelief for a quick moment. "Do you know where we can find him?"

"Yea, I know where to find him, but you'll never get to see him," Simon answered as he quickly adjusted he glasses nervously. "Nobody here has actually seen him. He's a bit of a mystery around here."

"What do you mean a mystery?" asked Thomas.

"Well," he started, "he sent a letter to the business office about two years ago wanting to rent the spare space in the basement of this building. It came, I hear, with a pretty handsome check. The manager agreed to rent the place and the newspaper's out dated printing equipment. The guy moved into the space a day later and started right to work on The Eerie Truth Weekly. But no one ever sees him come or go. It's as though he lives down there or something."

"What else can you tell me about him?" Tabby asked before Thomas could butt in.

"Not much really," Simon went on. "He stays to himself, never wants to be bothered, and orders a lot of pizza. He has it delivered to the hallway downstairs and leaves an envelope with cash at the door. Like I said, no one has ever seen him."

"OK then," Tabby said as she turned to face the others, "to the basement we go."

"But there is one minor little detail I might have forgotten to mention." Simon began to conclude. "There is only one way to get into the basement."

"Let me guess," April asked as she turned to peer into the window of the door they had just been chased out of. "Past Mr. Soldier-of-Fortune over there?"

"No, through the back stairway of the building. You either go through the main lobby, or through the back delivery door. But that door only opens from the inside." Simon replied with a weird smirk on his face.

"And let me guess," asked Tabby. "There is going to be a price for you letting us in the back?"

"Bingo!" answered Simon as his grin grew to the point it started to look painful.

The trio looked at each other cautiously for a quick moment, then asked nearly in unison, "Well, what?"

"You need to…" he paused as if to add to the suspense, but the look on his face seemed more like he was still formulating his bribe payment, and failing miserably. He opened his mouth as though to speak, then quickly closed it and began to look around as though he was looking for some sort of inspiration.

"You're new at this, aren't you?" asked April who was beginning to get impatient.

Simon looked squarely at April. "Oh, you think?"

"Well, let me see if I can help you." offered April, as she floated over to Simon's side and put her hand on his arm. "I'm kind of an expert when it comes to this kind of thing."

Simon looked extremely dumbfounded at this point. He began to speak but was quickly cut off.

"You see, most people fashion their bribes in order to fulfill their immediate needs, such as money, food, popularity, etc…" Simon attempted to speak again and was trumped for a second time as she pulled herself closer. "But you, I can tell you are a man of higher intellectual savvy, far smarter than the average Joe."

He thought for a moment, and then began to nod slowly as though she was on to something. Then he began to open his mouth and again was interrupted.

"You are a man that commands respect and admiration from your follow co-workers. A man who's worth to mankind is far above common subsidence, a true man of integrity."

At this point, Simon had all but given up trying to interrupt. April was, as always, winning the battle. All he could do at this point was sit back and wait for her to pause long enough to get in a word.

"So," she finally began to conclude as she turned to look at him face to face. "What could a handsome, intelligent stud-muffin like you possibly need from young, innocent little me?" she finished, batting her eyebrows, and pulling him closer to herself again.

Simon thought for a second, then began to speak, "Well, I was going to tell you to say please but, now that you mention it, a handsome, intelligent stud-muffin like me could stand to gain from this opportunity."

April could feel the other two staring at the back of her head. It felt strangely like one of the two, maybe both, was about to hit her with a large blunt object. But as always, she maintained nearly perfect composure and just looked up at Simon attentively.

"HHHHmmmmmm..." Simon thought to himself as he lightly tapped his fingers on his chin. He never once took his eyes off of Tabby for what seemed to be eternity before he finally pointed a finger at her. "How about you and me, Saturday night, double feature at the drive-in?"

Tabby felt ill struck. The idea of puking in her own mouth seemed like a reasonable and more entertaining alternative to having to be seen sitting next to this guy for even a minute, let alone three to four hours in a darkened drive-in theater. She inhaled quickly and deeply in preparation of a well-rounded verbal assault when without a single hesitation April intersected, "She'll do it!"

Tabby, stunned and confused, turned quickly to April with a look that in most cases could have been fatal.

"See you round back in five minutes!" April added quickly as she grabbed Thomas and Tabby's hands and began to walk quickly around the corner. Tabby was holding April's hand quite tightly, but at that moment, she was thinking of something else to wrap her fingers around.

Tabby waited until they were a short distance away before she was able to protest the terms of their agreement. "Are you insane?" Tabby whispered in a stern voice. "I wouldn't... couldn't... how could you..." Tabby had a problem getting complete sentences out when she became flustered. It was a condition her friends knew all too well.

"Don't get bent out of shape, I do have a plan to get you out of this," she began to explain before Tabby could begin to give her an earful of complaints. "Our main goal is to find Jerry before that dweeb opens the door."

Tabby was confused and quickly running out of breath. "How in the world does Jerry fit into this master plan of yours? You know if he's seen the word will get out, he will have no place to hide,"

"Trust me," April answered quickly as she practically dragged the other two round the corner and signaled for Jerry to come out of hiding. "If all goes as planned, this geek will never know what hit him."

Chapter 4

"No…no way…you expect me to…you are out of your …" Jerry stuttered in disbelief.

Thomas and April couldn't help but notice how similar both Jerry and Tabby act when they are put on the spot, It was kind of cute.

Jerry paced quickly back and forth nervously as he contemplated the implications of his actions if this plan didn't work. "This could turn out really bad."

"Relax, this plan is fool-proof. Besides, I hear him coming right now, hurry up!" April rushed as she turned Jerry around and shoved him towards the big iron door in front of them.

The door started to creak open slowly, Jerry took a deep breath in anticipation for what he was going to do. At this point, he truly believed that he was more scared than the guy was going to be. But to hesitate at this point would completely ruin any plans of getting in and finding out what had happened to him. He crouched down and waited for just the right moment.

Finally, the door flew open exposing a geeky looking fellow with a grin that stretched from ear to ear. Instantly Jerry leaped forward and let out a horribly deafening roar that even made the other three nearly jump out of their skins. He then slammed into the nerdy fellow, knocking him off his feet, and slammed him hard onto the floor just inside the door. The sheer look of complete and utter terror on Simon's poor face was monumental. He was shaking so bad he could hardly catch his breath. His mouth kept opening and closing as though to let out a scream, but all he could muster was a few pitiful whimpers at the sight of this horrible beast that was now crouched on top of him.

Jerry moved his face closer to Simon's to make sure he could see every detail. Then with an eerie growl he said, "If I ever find out you tried to take this young lady out against her will again, you will wish you were never born."

Simon nervously nodded as Jerry continued, "You will also accommodate their every request to access this door from now on."

Simon once again nodded, still too frightened to speak as Jerry concluded, "And last but not least, you will never speak of anything you witnessed tonight, including me, or it will be the last words you ever speak. Do I make myself clear?"

Simon finally was able to squeak out a high pitched "yes" as Jerry began to lift himself off of the quivering mass which remained on the floor.

"Go!" Jerry roared loudly as Simon quickly jumped to his feet and half ran, half stumbled out the back door and disappeared into the darkness of the alley. For about a minute or so, you could still hear Simon's stumbling, tripping, and whimpering.

The other three, in utter disbelief, slowly turned towards the rear door to find Jerry standing and holding the door open. "I hope this was the effect you were looking for, if not, I may have just psychologically damaged that man for life."

"Remind me not to piss you off," Thomas answered as the three entered the doorway.

"I would just as well not do that to another human being again," Jerry reassured him. "Also, I would steer clear of that puddle there."

The hallway in the basement leading to the door they wanted was dark and menacing. It was dimly lit by about three light bulbs in which two looked as though they were about to burn out. Piles of older issues of the local paper lined the hallways covered with about an inch of dust. The walls were bare other than a few bits of paper taped up containing employee memos that dated back quite a few years. The floors were covered in debris which made a crackling noise with every step.

"It looks as though nobody has been down here in years," Tabby remarked quietly to herself as they made their way down the corridor. "Someone should do something about this, it's a fire trap down here. Not to mention how many trees went to waste."

"Let's save the trees later," replied Jerry as they snaked their way around another pile of papers. "For now, can we concentrate on me?"

Tabby turned to Jerry ready to give him a piece of her mind, when all of a sudden, a loud noise echoed across the hallway like a door slamming. The four about jumped out of their skin and darted around looking for a place to hide. As the footsteps began to sound closer, everyone but Tabby had secured a spot. She began to panic when all of a sudden, she felt a hand reach around her waist and lift her off the floor. The unseen force spun her around and planted her against the wall along a darkened portion of the hallway, then felt a body press up against her. She opened her mouth to scream, but before she could, a huge hand covered her mouth as she heard a very faint, "ssshhh!"

She looked up to see Jerry's deformed face just inches away from hers. She was relieved for a short time until the source of the footsteps came into view. It was a young man Tabby recognized from her school. He was dressed in a pizza delivery uniform and holding two large boxes of pizza. He knocked on the door, placed the pizzas on the floor, picked up an envelope, checked the contents, knocked again, and left without a word. The two looked at each other in unison then checked to see if the coast was clear. Within seconds, the door opened. From the entrance of the doorway a stick, with a hook on the end, probed its way out. The hook slid around the pizza boxes, pulled the boxes inside, them immediately the door slammed shut again. The slam was then followed by a short series of five or six clicks as though someone was barricading the door shut.

Tabby was finally able to exhale. She hadn't even been aware that she was holding her breath. She thought for another moment about the fact that the most popular boy in school had her pressed against the wall and was not letting go. Quickly she shoved him back, looked at him for another brief moment. Then dusted herself off and turned as though nothing was wrong. "That was too close." She said to break the awkward moment.

She didn't like him that way even a little bit, and she was determined to make sure he knew it to. *Not that he would ever be interested in me when he had his pick of just about any girl he wanted*, she quietly thought to herself.

"Tell me about it," Thomas agreed as he and April began to rise from their hiding spots and began dusting themselves off as well.

"So, why would someone not just come out to grab the boxes?" Jerry asked as he peered down the hallway to the anonymous door.

Tabby turned and stared at the door as well. "Somebody who really wants to keep themselves hidden from the rest of the world, I guess."

"Perhaps we've found Quazy's missing look-a-like?" April inquired.

"Or worse," Thomas finished as the foursome slowly made their way to the front of the door.

The door was big and heavy looking. There were no signs that anything important was inside. The only clue that gave away the fact that they had found the place they wanted was the small pile of mail littering the floor in front of the door which were addressed to the small tabloid paper.

The group looked at each other to see who was going to knock, Tabby finally stepped forward. "Fine...I'll do it!"

She gave the door three good solid knocks, and then waited, but no one answered or replied. She knocked three more times, still no answer. She was beginning to lose her patience. "I know someone is in there, I saw the door close!"

"Go away! You're not welcome here!" yelled a voice from the other side of the door, which sounded as though the person had food in his mouth.

"We need to see Glimpin Dimbwick, it is very important!" Tabby yelled to the unknown voice behind the door.

After a brief pause the voice sounded out again, this time closer to the door and free from food. "Not to me it's not! Now scram!"

The others could see Tabby's face begin to turn red at this point, she was going to burst at the seams, but for the time being was maintaining her composure. "Please, my friend here is in trouble, we need your help!"

"The only help you need is learning the English language. Let me see if I can help. Scram, beat it, leave, depart, move along, get out of here, any of this sinking in?" screamed the voice from the other side of the door. "I got better things to do than cater to a group of teenage, pimple faced punks so get lost!"

"That's it!" yelled Jerry as he reared up and charged towards the door.

Tabby was just barely out of the way before he struck the door with his shoulder and blasted the door open. As the dust began to settle, a shadow quickly blitzed across the door opening and flew behind a pile of pizza boxes on the other side of the room. "Are you stinking crazy?" the voice yelled.

Tabby entered the room next to survey the scene. "I don't know what you got going on here, but we have questions, and by god you are going to an…swer…them…?"

Tabby was frozen, she couldn't move a single muscle. She was completely in shock at what she was looking at. Jerry had just gotten up and turned when he too had to stop and stare. "What on earth is…"

Tabby remained still, her eye were fixed on what only could be the most amazing thing she had ever seen. After a moment or two, she could only manage to get one word out. "Sketchy?"

In front of them standing about six feet tall was what looked like a stick figure, drawn in mid-air, slowly standing up with its arms in the air. It had a line for a body, lines for its arms, legs, and neck, and completed with a slightly out-of-round circle for a head.

Thomas and April walked in just at that moment and paused as well. Both were completely blown away at the sight.

"Is that thing real?" Thomas asked as he stopped in his tracks.

"He is real!" Tabby answered. She began to feel a little faint. Her legs felt numb as she began to drop down to her knees. As she knelt down she looked to see where she was dropping to when she noticed a dog cautiously creep up to her.

She began to reach out her hand to reassure the pooch that she was friendly. "It's OK, I'm not going to hurt you," she said in a soft voice as not to scare it.

As the dog came closer into the light when she made a terrifying discovery that quickly sent her back to her feet, scaring the dog who turned and ran back to its hiding place screeching like a bat. The dog had wings like a bat sticking out of its back.

"Oh my god, it's all real," Tabby discovered as her eyes began to adjust to the low light and could see everything. There were notes, photographs, and newspaper excerpts covering nearly every inch of wall in the room. The counter space which circled around the room was littered with all sorts of tools and empty pizza boxes, along with an old fashioned spy glass and a Polaroid camera. She could see in the next room mounds of paper and an old style printing press. The floor was covered with wadded up newspapers and half eaten pizza crust.

"Of course it's real you dingbat! Why else would I call it The Eerie Truth Weekly, and not the Hey! I just made up this garbage so as to entertain you lame brains! Now you've already seen too much so get out!" said the voice from behind another stack of boxes.

Tabby began to walk slowly towards the sound of the voice, "We're sorry about the door but-"

"Not as sorry as you're going to be if you don't leave right now!" the voice yelled again as it started to finally make its way out from behind the boxes and into view.

He was about four feet tall, slightly plump, with rosy cheeks and a big fat nose which protruded prominently above a snow white beard. He was wearing an all red suit and a pointed hat that stood almost as tall as he was. He crouched down slightly and wielded what looked like a cricket bat. "I won't give you another warning!"

"He's an elf?!" Thomas shouted from behind the group.

"You idiot," April began to answer. "He quite clearly is a gnome."

The gnome slowly began to rear the bat. "That's it, I warned you!"

"Wait!" Jerry slid forward in front of Tabby just as he was ready to swing. "Please, just tell me what is happening to me, please."

The gnome stopped in mid swing and looked at Jerry for a brief moment. "Acne?" it answered as it brought the bat back up and prepared to swing again.

"He didn't look like this at all three days ago!" Tabby tried to explain. "He was tall, slender, and hand… well…not like this."

"Then go see a doctor!" the gnome snapped back.

Tabby was beginning to get fed up with this argument. "Look, you know something and I'm not leaving until I get answers!"

The gnome looked at the pair angrily, then after a few short moments exhaled and dropped the bat to his side. "Get away from the door."

The group walked further away from the doorway. The gnome strolled over to the splintered remains of the door kneeled down and put a hand on the door. Just under its breath they could hear him softly mumble something, then instantly the door flew off the ground, pieced itself back together and returned to the doorway good as new.

The group was speechless as the gnome turned to face them. "I am Glimpin Dimbwick, I am a gnome, and your friend there, is cursed."

Chapter 5

"What do you mean cursed?" asked Tabby as she desperately looked for an available seat, with a dreadful feeling that this explanation was going to take a while.

Glimpin sighed as he turned his head slightly, whistled, and began to sit down as several chairs slid across the floor and rested just behind each person in the room. "I guess the best way to explain it is to start from the beginning…"

"Hundreds of years ago in medieval England, mystical creatures still roamed the English countryside. Dragons, elves, dwarfs, orcs, all sorts of creatures lived peacefully amongst each other in an area known as the Forbidden Lands, well away from human kind. The area was protected by a magical tree known as Ryho. Ryho was protected by a magical barrier that was created by The Great Stone Gateway."

"The Gateway was a circle of stone pillars with a single stone altar in the middle. It was said that those who entered the Gateway could see the tree which was invisible to everyone else."

"Hold on," interrupted Thomas. "Are you talking about Stonehenge?"

Glimpin looked at Thomas for a moment. "Yes, genius, I'm talking about Stonehenge."

"OK, now I know you're full of it. Everyone knows that Stonehenge was used for pagan rituals and sacrifices." Thomas replied as he crossed his arms in front of his chest with a smart look on his face.

Glimpin looked at him with a puzzled look on his face. "So you knew ten minutes ago that gnomes were real? That a stick figure drawing could walk? Or do you think that your friend here is just having some weird allergic reaction to fast food. Perhaps the reality you humans have created over the years is nothing more than your own illusions, and that perhaps those mysteries in this world that can't be explained, are exactly what they seem."

Thomas sank back into his seat looking a bit chagrined, Then nodded for Glimpin to continue.

"Anyways," Glimpin continued. "From time to time, a human would wander along, get scared out of their pants, and then return to their village telling stories of unspeakable horrors and monsters, mostly untrue. In time, they would send out soldiers to eradicate the supposed threat. Most of the human soldiers were scared off or killed before they could reach the Gateway."

"And this is relevant to our friends condition why?" asked April from the back of the room.

"Hey! You wanted answers so stop interrupting!" Glimpin snarled back. "Now let me finish."

"So for hundreds of years there were ongoing battles between mankind and the inhabitants of the Forbidden Lands, until Corum came around. Corum was a dangerous wizard who was bent on destroying the trees powers, as to unleash a darker power, subdued power by Ryho, and to rule the world with it.

So he and his hordes found and attacked the Gateway. It was a massacre, the inhabitants of the Forbidden Lands were no match for the army, the Gateway was partly damaged and its power to protect Ryho was lost."

Glimpin continued. "But what Corum didn't know is that Ryho was nowhere near the Gateway, not even the same continent. After the battle was lost, a few of the inhabitants were able to escape the horde army and made their way to the last place on earth they thought they could be found which was at the actual location of Ryho."

Tabby was sure of what her answer would be, but asked anyways. "So where was Ryho?"

Glimpin sighed, "In a little area later to be known as..." He paused as though he shouldn't answer, "Eerie County."

Everyone sat silent for a moment, and then Thomas broke the silence again. "So how did a band of wayward mystical creatures from England get all the way over here?"

"The Gateway could be used as a portal," Glimpin explained, "Just before the Gateway lost all its power, they slipped through the portal undetected. Of course Corum was furious, and sent his scouts to all the ends of the Earth looking for it. Without the protection of the Gateway, it didn't take long for him to find it and he mounted one last offensive to destroy Ryho's powers."

"Then what happened?" asked Jerry, who was now sitting Indian style on the floor in front of Glimpin like a kindergartner.

Glimpin sighed again. "He was only able to take a few soldiers to the second fight. He did win, the last of the mystical creatures were obliterated or scattered to the ends of the Earth, but not without suffering fatal injuries himself. Fearing that he was dying, he ordered Ryho to be cut down and burned."

April sat up straight on her stool. "That seemed a little harsh, cut down a tree so nobody else could use it."

"Well, as legend would have it, Corum died, Ryho was cut down, and was burned to ashes, or so they thought." Glimpin continued, "Not all of Ryho was torched. A major portion of the tree's main trunk would not burn. So it was ground down into pulp and made into thirteen separate scrolls, known then as the "Scrolls of Corum" in the wizards honor. Only a select few truly knew what the scrolls could really do though."

"What can the scrolls do?" asked Tabby in a fearful voice, thinking they were getting close to an answer to Jerry's affliction.

"From my research, I've been able to narrow it down to three major powers. The First, if a picture is drawn on the scrolls and moistened by the waters of Dead Man's Lake, then the picture will come to life. That's how Sketchy came to be." He answered as he turned and pointed at the poor stick figure standing behind him. "A little boy happened upon a piece of the scroll in Butcher's Forest after swimming in the lake, enough said."

"The Second power allows the person with the scroll to alter or change someone else's appearance. Draw a picture of whatever and add a few drops of blood from the victim on to it, and that person becomes whatever was drawn. That is what is wrong with your friend here. But the ultimate purpose of the Scrolls of Corum is to drain the remaining power from the root of the mystic tree. Right now, the root's purpose is to keep mankind from discovering the truth of the real world around them. But, the root is dying, using the scrolls only help to speed up the process."

Thomas scratched his head for a quick moment, "Who would nowadays know how to use the scrolls, and why would they be after Jerry? He's just a regular teenager in high school."

"I don't know, but you have seven days from the time the curse was cast in order to figure it out before his condition becomes permanent," Glimpin replied as he stood up from his chair. "You have got to keep this a secret. As long as people think that Sketchy, Fang and others like them are just figments of a tabloid writer's wild imagination, they can remain hidden and safe."

"That's why you write <u>The Eerie Truth Weekly</u>, to beat possible witnesses to the punch so others will write them off as nonsense?" Tabby asked.

Glimpin nodded. "And to draw out the person who has the remaining scrolls. I have five out of the thirteen. Problem is that whoever has the others has been chopping them up, there could be a lot more pieces than there were before."

"Then we better get going home." April said as she turned around and gave Fang a little pat on the head. "Tomorrow's Friday, we only have two days tops to find out who's behind this."

Glimpin grabbed Tabby's hand as she turned to walk out with the others. She turned quickly and looked down at the Gnome who peered up at her. "There is one more thing you need to know before you start this."

"What is that?"

"One, the Caster cannot be the artist nor can the artist be the Caster. And the Caster cannot possess the scroll once cast. This means there is more than one person you're looking for.

"You mentioned three powers the scrolls had, what is the third?" Tabby asked after everyone left the room.

Glimpin hesitated for a moment. "If the Caster tricks or convinces someone into signing the scroll with their full birth name bestowed by their maternal mother, they will become a slave to the Caster for as long as they live, even if the scroll or the Caster is destroyed. This makes the slaves, or servants as they are called, even more dangerous than the Caster themselves. A Caster cannot kill or they will lose their power."

"How do we reverse Jerry's curse after we find the scroll?"

"You leave that part to me." Glimpin said as he motioned for her to leave.

"How will we get back in here to see you again?"

Glimpin handed her a piece of stick. "Wave this in front of any wooden door and it will open for you. I will meet you by Slasher's Hills tomorrow night at dusk. See what you find out between now and then," he paused again. "And one last thing, now that you guys know the truth, things you've taken for granted will become visible to you. I have never trusted anyone with this knowledge before. I am counting on you guys to not make me regret it."

"I have to help Jerry, no matter what the stakes. You can trust me, your secret is safe with me."

Chapter 6

Tabby, Thomas, April and Jerry stood in silence outside of the newspaper building's back door for several minutes before Thomas spoke. "I'm beginning to wonder if we aren't in over our heads on this, I think we need to call the cops."

"Are you nuts?" Tabby asked as she turned to face him. "If we call the cops, everything we just seen and heard will crack wide open, everyone will know and…"

"And it won't be our problem anymore." Thomas finished. "This isn't a game anymore, or one of your mediocre adventures, this is serious magic and serious danger. I would love to help Jerry out, but to what end? We are nothing but a bunch of teenagers, how can we possibly fight against an unknown enemy who has knowledge of an evil ancient magic that we can't defend against? It's suicide."

"We have to try!" Tabby shot back. "Jerry doesn't deser-"

"Jerry doesn't what?" Thomas interrupted "deserve this?! He barely speaks to you in like years, now he deserves for you and us to risk our lives for what? So you can swap stupid sandwiches in secret behind the school building for the rest of your high school career. What do you owe this guy? Nothing!"

Jerry lowered his head. "He's right," Jerry turned and lunged into the darkness of the back alleyway and disappeared.

"Jerry wait!" Tabby yelled as he disappeared then turned sharply and looked into Thomas's eyes. She was not happy at all. "You are a jerk!"

"He does make a good point," April added as she walked up and put a comforting hand on Tabby's shoulder.

"That's not the point!" Tabby continued.

"Then what is it?" Thomas asked. "Why does he deserve our help?"

"Because right now, right here, we are the only help he's got. No one would believe our story if we did tell. And last, he doesn't have to deserve help to get it. That is what separates us from the rest of the cattle at school. If we do nothing, we would be as bad as them. Do you think any of his so called friends are going to jump in and help? Most of them are self-centered morons worried more about self-image and popularity. If they cared, maybe they would have checked on him first."

"And what makes you think he's any different? Jerry is about as bad as the rest of them." Thomas shot back. "Are you sure there isn't some other reason why you're ready to throw your life away for him?"

"No! There's not!" Tabby shouted "Besides, if this could happen to him, you or I or anyone else could be next. We have to stop it!"

"Don't say we." Thomas said quietly as he turned and started to walk away. "I am not going to be a part of this."

Tabby stared unbelievingly at Thomas as he walked away. She felt I tear start to form from her eye. *I can't believe he just walked away like that.* She thought to herself.

"He's liked you for a while you know?" April said from behind her. "I'm sure he just doesn't want you to get hurt."

"He knows where I stand April. I don't like him that way."

"And Jerry?"

"No, all I know is that helping him is the right thing to do, no matter what, with or without him," she turned and faced April. "I take it you're out too?"

"Heck no girl, I am way in!" April said in a cheery voice which helped lighten Tabby's mood. "But if I get killed, I'm haunting your butt for the rest of your life. Besides, all this talk about other worldly creatures and magic has me way too excited to turn back now."

"Thanks April, you're a true friend."

The trip home was quiet. April left to go home and get some rest. Tabby was on her way as well. Something was different though, everything seemed weird to her. The trees along the sides the streets seemed more crooked than usual. It was darker, more eerie than normal.

Maybe I just never noticed before. She thought to herself.

"Thomas is right." Jerry said from behind Tabby. Tabby for some reason had known he was close. She just stopped walking, and listened as Jerry continued. "I have been a real jerk to you guys since junior high began. I had written you guy off since I started making new friends, I didn't even acknowledge your presence when we met outside."

"None of that matters, people-"

"It does matter to me! I don't want you thinking you need to risk your life for my sake, I don't deserve it."

Tabby turned and lifted his chin to meet her gaze. "Friends grow apart all the time, it's no big deal. It doesn't mean we stop caring, and it doesn't make me feel less obliged to help you. I may not care too much for your new set of friends, but

I still care about you, and the memories of us hanging out as children. I still remember the time you put gum in my hair and smashed eggs in my shirt pockets."

Jerry smiled, "That was pretty funny, you cried for hours."

They shared a laugh together for a brief moment.

"I don't want you getting hurt on my account. Promise me you won't try something stupid without me there, and when push comes to shove, get away and let me handle it. I don't know if I could live with myself if something happened to you."

Tabby felt a moment coming on. She quickly helped him finish his sentence as she took half a step back. "Or April right? I mean, she is helping to."

Jerry giggled. "Relax, Tabby. Yes, April either."

"Good."

"Good."

Jerry turned and offered to walk Tabby the rest of the way home, covered of course, Tabby accepted. Now she just had to come up with a good excuse why Thomas wouldn't be with her when she got home.

Chapter 7

The next morning Tabby woke up about a half hour earlier than normal. She felt compelled to get to school early and start snooping around for any evidence to who might be behind Jerry's curse. She was up half the night thinking about the possibilities. It occurred to her that if anyone had a motive to help someone hurt Jerry. It would have to be someone from school.

Of course the only way to get close enough to everyone else in school was to mingle with the others that she, until now, really could have cared less about. This, of course, made Tabby's stomach turn to think she was going to have to join the herd for even a single day. But it was for the best if she was going to get to the bottom of this.

To make herself more acceptable she put on some newer, little more fashionable clothing. It consisted of a poke-a-dotted form fitting tank top, short skirt, and panty hose. But the one thing she hated most of all about the outfit. It was the worst color in Tabby's world, pink.

She was really feeling out of her element, but pushed forward out the door where she found April waiting in the wings as normal, besides the sight of her jaw dropping nearly to her waist.

"OMG! Girl, you are looking fine today! Why the sudden interest in clothing? Or did you get lucky and find these nice cloths at the thrift store?" April commented as they started walking down the sidewalk.

Tabby answered quietly. "All I'm going to say is somebody better appreciate this if all goes well."

"He better, and every other guy that catch a glimpse of you in that dress today. Let me guess, you think someone at school has something to do with Jerry's little transformation? So you're dressing up to blend in with the hordes of the brain dead to find out if anyone has any information." April asked.

"Bingo," Tabby answered as she looked around, "No Thomas today, huh?"

"Bingo," April echoed as they began to cross the street about a block from Thomas's house.

"Should we stop by on our way?" Tabby asked.

"Umm, no," April replied. "I think he's having a hard time keeping the heart in his chest without seeing you in this fine getup. Think you better just let him simmer down from yesterday, he'll come around."

"You're probably right," replied Tabby as they walked closer and closer to Thomas's house, which happened to be at the corner where they caught the bus. But when they got there, there was still no sign of Thomas.

Is he not going to school today? Thought Tabby as she looked around the corner and saw the bus coming from down the road.

"You're moving to the back of the bus for once?" April asked as the bus pulled up to the girls.

"As far back as I can stand before I feel the need to slap someone," murmured Tabby as the doors opened.

"This is going to be a very long day for you, sweetie," April predicted as the two stepped up onto the bus.

It didn't take long for the normal volume of the calamity in the back of the bus to lower as more and more guys stopped for a moment and stared. Tabby started to blush a little as she brushed a few strands of hair out of her face and slowly worked her way towards the back of the bus. April stopped her about half way back and immediately sat her down in the nearest seat.

"What are you doing? I was halfway there," Tabby whispered as she rubbed her butt after crashing down on the hard seat.

April replied in a similar voice. "One, baby steps, let the men come to you. Second, Thomas just climbed aboard and does not look happy," she then quickly raised her head looking straight behind Tabby. "Hello," she said as she nodded to Tabby to take a look for herself.

Tabby quickly turned and saw the rather cute looking boy standing behind her. She normally would have already gathered about a dozen different "get lost" phases by now and picked the worse. But instead just held her tongue and looked dumbfounded as to what to say.

The boy leaned over slightly and placed his hand on the back of Tabby's seat. "Are you new here? Or am I so shallow as to never have noticed you before?" The boy asked as the bus started to move.

Tabby thought hard for a brief moment, then let the first thing slip out of her mouth that came to mind. "Well... admitting you have a problem with shallowness is the first step towards recovery."

The boy laughed. "Well, imagine that, beautiful and witty. I do feel inspired to sit with you and hear more about my optional treatment plans for my ailment, but perhaps we may instead sit together at lunch this afternoon and discuss this further."

"Um, sure," Tabby squeaked out as the boy turned and walked back to the seat a few rows behind them and sat down, never taking his eyes off of her.

April looked at Tabby with her head slightly tilted to the right. "Next time I get to wear the dress."

"This isn't a social call, I need to infiltrate Jerry's group of friends quickly if I'm going to get any clues," Tabby reminded her. "Who was that anyways?"

"That's Zack McClure. He's on the varsity football team," she paused for a moment. "Not too bad, you managed to reeled in the second string quarterback for the varsity football team in the first outing as a normal teenage girl, I'm impressed."

Tabby shot back, "I'm not interested in anybody! I just want some answers, that's all."

"Girl, you're weird. How are you going to let a fine man like him get by you? Maybe you need to loosen up a little. Not every man in high school is a Neanderthal. Besides look at you, you're a beautiful young lady. You need to go shopping at some real stores for once," April paused again as Tabby looked at her then put her head down.

April sighed, "Look, let's just get to the bottom of this mess, and when this whole deal with Jerry is done and he's off butting heads with the rest of the bulls, me and you will go out and get a nice makeover like regular teenage girlfriends do, how does that sound?"

"I guess that could be nice." Tabby answered as she lifted her head and smiled. "But I still refuse to let anyone get me sucked into some stupid, brainless clique."

"Don't worry," April assured her, "I know you all too well. Fitting in is not your style, but it don't mean you can't look good swatting at the flies in this school."

"So you plan on following through with this!" a voice rang out from the seat in front of them. "You're going to get hurt or killed if you do this."

Tabby leaned forward in her seat closer to the one in front of her. "I don't care Thomas you're not talking me out of this."

"Is it that important to you to throw your life away, or is he?" Thomas asked.

"Both..." she couldn't believe she had just said that.

"That's what I thought," Thomas said in a disappointing voice.

"That's not what I meant!" Tabby shot back.

There was a long silence, long miserable silence that lingered in the air with a slight hint of discomfort.

"Jerry got into an argument with your new boyfriend there last week over the fact that Jerry was going to move up as the varsity quarterback position next year instead of moving up the secondary position. It was pretty heated from what I was told. Maybe you should try there first."

Tabby leaned back in her seat again. "Thanks Thomas. I knew I could count on you."

Again, another long silence before Thomas spoke again. "You look nice today by the way."

"Don't get used to it and get your tongue back in your mouth." Tabby returned as she smiled and closed her eyes for the rest of the trip to school.

She started to think to herself. *Jerry wouldn't go for me anyways, I'm too smart.* Tabby wasn't sure why she just thought that. She wouldn't really want Jerry to go for her at all. She quickly diminished the thought and concentrated on the task at hand.

Tabby felt awkward that day. Things just didn't seem right to her, and it wasn't just because of the conforming outfit or her mother's makeup that she never wore before. The school itself seemed, dreary. The hallways seemed darker than usual, and less straight. The lockers that lined the halls seemed crooked, the floor a little less polished. To be honest, even the other students and teachers seemed a little off.

Then she thought back to what Glimpin had told her the night before, ...*Now that you guys know the truth, things you've taken for granted will become visible to you.* Was this what he was talking about? Surprisingly, it got worse as the day went on. It wasn't until lunch when her assumed reality would really take its true form.

As she walked into the cafeteria, she was stopped in her tracks. Everyone was carrying on like nothing was wrong, but everything had changed to her eyes. Some students clothing looked as though they had just crawled out a dirty grave. Their faces slightly deformed as though they were made of putty. The food looked grey and inedible. Chairs and tables sat crooked and unbalanced as other students ate. It all seemed really, eerie.

She turned quickly to jet back out the door and ran directly into another student. *Great!* She thought to herself, *It's that Zack guy.*

"Leaving so soon, beautiful? I thought I just saw you come in here a second ago.

Tabby looked up and noticed that he hadn't changed compared to the other students in the school. She thought quickly to herself for a moment. "Umm...I sort of forgot something important I needed to do."

Zack turned his head sideways and looked at Tabby with a weird grin. "So, what could be more important that meeting me for lunch?"

Tabby dug deep trying to come up with an answer. "Umm... I forgot I was supposed to be getting homework together for a friend. He's been sick all week. Excuse me."

She tried to maneuver around Zack but was cut off quickly. "Who's your friend, if I may ask?"

Tabby avoided looking at Zack as she decided this would be a great opportunity to start steering the conversation in the right direction. "Jerry."

The look on Zack's face couldn't have changed from curious to angry fast enough as he took a deep breath and began to speak again. "Jerry Patterson? The freshman quarterback of the J.V. squad who thinks he has what it takes to be varsity. I had no idea he had such a considerate friend."

Tabby looked up at Zack and shrugged her shoulders. "I guess that's what good friends are for. Excuse me," she attempted to walk away again, but was once again cut off before she could make her escape.

"So, have you seen Mr. Patterson this week? I was told that he wasn't quite feeling like himself," Zack asked as he straightened up and looked around the room like he was looking for someone.

"No, I mean yes, yes I have seen him. He just has the flu. He told me he would be back on Monday for sure," Tabby said quickly. She was beginning to feel nervous. He was giving off a really weird vibe that was overwhelming.

"So... you and him an item huh?" he asked as he looked down at her as though she had just done something wrong.

"Oh, no," Tabby added quickly. "No, not us, no. What would make you say that?"

"No reason, just curious to see if I had any competition for taking you out tonight."

Tabby just stood there for a moment wondering how to get out of this situation. She wanted to throw him across the room for making her sound like some first place prize, and yet felt even more compelled to puke. "Well, I will probably be helping him do his homework tonight, so probably not."

Zack looked at her in a very disappointed tone. "OK, I will take that as a rain check then?"

"Yes! A rain check, definitely a rain check then," she answered as she finally made it around Zack and started down the hallway. But as quickly as she got around him she felt a hand grab her arm. It was Zack who had started to lean close to the side of her head.

"Are you sure he only has the flu? Or is he hiding the fat lip I gave him last week?"

"You two were in a fight?"

"Not really, we just had a little discussion about his rightful place on the varsity football team next year. Let's just say he knows his place now," he slowly straightened up and adjusted his jacket. "Tell him Zack says hi, and that I'll be seeing him again about the blood stain on my shirt," He chuckled for a moment. "Poor kid never even fought back, talk about a loser."

Zack walked away. "I'm telling you beautiful, you're better off without him."

Tabby stared at Zack as he walked away. "Jerry could have ripped him apart, why didn't he?"

More importantly, Tabby now knew who would have had a motive, and how he would have gotten the blood for the scroll. Now she just needed to figure out where the scroll was. But she couldn't help but wonder why Jerry wouldn't have fought back in their fight, and why he didn't mention it to her the other night. Something else was going on, and she was going to get to the bottom of it.

Chapter 8

It was getting close to dusk. Tabby and April were standing at the base of Slasher's Hills. Both had spent the afternoon discussing the weird things they had been seeing all day long. April seemed strangely calm about the sudden change in their immediate environment. When asked about her rock steady acceptance to her surroundings, she simply stated that it was cool as long as her perfect complexion still smiled back at her in the mirror. She could be a little self-centered and conceited at times.

"Thomas is still a no show huh?" asked Tabby as she sat at the base of the hill, feeling much more comfortable in her own clothes.

April sat right next to her and lay back with her arms crossed behind her. "Guess he's too scared to have an adventure. So, you think this Zack guy had something to do with Jerry's predicament?"

"Maybe, all the pieces seem to fit, and something about him doesn't seem right," Tabby answered as she thought back to the conversation from earlier.

"Personally, I think you're creating unreasonable conclusions. I mean really, a high school student, a jock no less involved in the occult," April explained as she turned and looked at Tabby with a weird look on her face. "Maybe you're on the wrong trail. We should consider other avenues first."

"No," Tabby answered. "After the conversation this afternoon, I'm more certain Zack has to be in on this, somehow."

"Anywho, how was the rest of your day as a hot chick?" April smirked as she turned on her side to face Tabby.

Tabby frowned. "It had to be the most humiliating day in my life. I mean, I've been going to that school for my entire life, and it took a form-fitting dress and contacts to get me noticed by anyone. Has our society really sunk to such low levels that the only way to be part of this world is to conform to the shallow minded minions of the media stereotypes? Furthermore, why do I have to flaunt my assets, can people not see the person I am and just be happy, besides you and Thomas? You two are like the only sane people left in this god forsaken town."

"Sanity is irrelevant in this place. They only lock up the dangerous ones," April replied. "But you didn't answer my question."

"And there is a good reason for that. I got hit on by about half the football and basketball teams, had about a hundred useless conversations with other girls regarding where I got my dress and where I should go for the best deals on lacy panties and manicures, and a quick meeting with a teacher who wasn't quite sure who I was," Tabby answered.

April giggled. "Sounds like you had a pretty normal day to me, you'll get used to it."

"I think not," Tabby quickly answered. "Monday, I'm back to invisible mode again."

"Oh, you're no fun," April replied as she sat up.

"Did I miss something?" a voice called out from behind the girls, who let out a shriek. It was only Jerry.

"Ever hear of a warning or a knock, or maybe walking up from the front?" April snapped.

"Sorry, kind of getting used to this sneaking around thing," Jerry said apologetically. "So what fun did I miss?"

"You missed the sight of a life time. Our little Tabby looked particularly hot today in school. Got it on my phone, want to see?" April replied as she pulled out her phone and pulled up the picture to show him.

"WOW!" Jerry replied, "How'd you get her to dress up in that?"

"She did that all by herself so she could get close to your friends at school to get some information."

Jerry looked stunned for a moment. "You dressed up like that for me?"

Tabby felt a blush coming on. "Don't get all mushy on me. I only did it to go undercover, and I have no intentions of ever doing it again, so don't ask."

Jerry shook his head and recomposed himself. "Ah, um, I really didn't mean anything by it, really. But if it means all the same to you, thank you. But the important question is did you find anything out?"

"Actually I did get some info, but first the burning question in my head is why did you not plow Zack McClure into the ground when he started throwing his weight around with you?" Tabby asked with a concerned look on her face.

Jerry lowered his head for a second, and then lifted it up high as though he had no regrets. "Fighting Zack would not change anything. Like I told him when he confronted me, I have no intentions on doing anything but what is best for the team. If the coach wants me in, I'm there. If he wants me to be secondary, I'm there. Zack's actions only make him look like a jerk. My finishing the fight would have only caused animosity within the team. I earn my stripes with hard work, not intimidation. If that makes me an outcast, so be it."

Tabby felt her heart flutter. It was the second time she'd felt it, and both times were in his presents. She quickly shrugged it off. "No, you're not a loser, Jerry. In fact, I kind of respect you a little bit more for showing restraint. It takes a good, strong person to do that, even if others don't see it."

"Thanks."

"No prob."

April looked at the two for a moment then felt the need to break into the conversation. "Personally I would have knocked his head off, but anyways, was there anything weird going on while you two were having your heated debate? Was anyone with you or him?"

"No," Jerry said as he did his best to recall the situation. "It was just him and me behind the school as I was leaving from detention. It was weird that I was the only one in detention that day though, usually at least three or four others are in there with me."

Tabby thought for a moment. "Why were you in detention?"

"What are you, my mom?!" he shot back, "What does any of this have to do with me looking like this? I just-"

Tabby shot back quickly, "I am trying to establish a link between the events leading, to and resulting, in your deformity. That's all. But I need to know all the details before I can come to a conclusion. So humor me, why were you in detention?"

Jerry sighed for a moment. "You know that idiot substitute teacher that is always scratching his ear?"

"Mr. Spader? Yes. He's been a substitute teacher for years. He's really mean." April answered.

Jerry continued. "Well, he caught me running in the halls between classes. I was late and was in a hurry. I accidently bumped into him and he sent me to detention."

"When did this happen?" Tabby asked.

"Wednesday," he replied.

Tabby thought to herself, then asked, "Don't you usually have detention the same day you are given it? Why would he wait till Friday?"

"I don't know, maybe because he's mean and wanted me to have to wait another hour before leaving for the weekend."

"Or he needed you to be alone when you and Zack 'accidently' happened to run into each other."

"Oh my god!" April replied, "It was the butler! I mean come on girl, are you sure this isn't just a bad case of coincidence?"

"Shh… I'm thinking," Tabby interrupted as she had to put things together in her mind. "Were you bleeding after the fight?"

"Maybe," Jerry replied. "Maybe a little, but I don't recall him or anyone else trying to collect it."

A rough, scratchy voice suddenly spoke from behind them. "It only takes one or two drops to do the job."

The three turned suddenly to see Glimpin standing a few yards away. He was dressed in a khaki colored cloak and a hat that was way too big for his head. Clearly it was to hide his long ears.

"Finally, you're here," April said in relief. "We have a lot of questions. Like what the heck is happening around here? Everything looks like it's been hit by a tornado and almost everyone by the ugly stick."

Glimpin sighed for a moment. "Nothing happened to them, something happened to you. It started when you blockheads decided to bust down my door, and as time goes by, it will happen even more."

"So what is happening?" asked Tabby as she stood up walked over to Glimpin and kneeled down near him.

"Look, the root of the mystic tree is dying, that spell on your friend here is sucking the life out of it. That root is what makes this whole area seem normal. But in fact, things in this town are very different. As it loses energy, it loses its ability to mask the true reason why this place is called Eerie County. Now that you know the truth, your veil has been lifted, and you now can see exactly what the people and places around here really look like. You know that old saying that beauty is only skin deep? Now you get to see people for who they really are, while they themselves stay completely oblivious of their own true projections."

"But the most important power the root holds is the power to hold back the true evil power that the Caster is really after. Although certain elements have to be in place before he can conjure up that power."

Tabby thought for a second. "Did you come up with any new information regarding who might be the Caster?"

"I'm afraid not. Whoever it is, they are fighting tooth and nail to keep themselves hidden. I've been following the same guy for years, but I have no idea who he is. Have you found anything on your end at the high school?"

"A couple of wild ideas, but nothing concrete yet," Tabby answered.

"Is it any more wild than having a vampire pooch at your feet?" Glimpin replied.

Tabby reached down and gave Fang a quick scratch behind the ears. "Jerry got into a fight at school last week with an upper classman from school. It's the only time he can think of that he may have been bleeding."

"He was alone at the school that afternoon because he was at detention for another incident, but the substitute teacher who put him there had him there alone. I sort of gathered that maybe the sub put him in detention by himself on purpose to ensure no one would be there when he and this guy ran into each other after detention was over."

"Sounds solid to me, we need to get more information about this substitute teacher, he must be our Caster," Glimpin said with confidence.

"But what about Zack, why would he be helping out an old buzzard like Mr. Spader?" April probed as she felt the need to throw in her own two cents worth.

"Maybe this Mr. Spader guy tricked Zack into signing the scroll making him a relentless servant," Tabby answered.

"In that case," Glimpin said with a hint of fear in his voice. "We must be very careful about dealing with him. He will be more dangerous than the Caster."

"Why is that?" asked Jerry who had tried to stay out of the conversation till now.

"The servant will follow any order the Caster gives them to the letter, even if they're asked to kill. If this Caster is as determined as Corum was, he will, and without hesitation."

"He seems like a big enough idiot to sign something like that. But it still doesn't explain why they targeted Jerry and not some other high school sap," April asked.

Jerry shook his head for a moment and turned to April with a look to kill. "Who are you calling a sap miss think-I'm-perfect-in-every-way-when-I'm-really-just-a-snob?"

April inhaled quickly, ready to unleash a borage of verbal insults when Tabby quickly cut them off. "Cut it out!"

Glimpin added quickly, "Tabby's right you two. We got other things to worry about than bickering amongst ourselves. We would only be wasting valuable time. We got about a day before Jerry's condition becomes permanent."

April exhaled quickly and stood up. "Fine, but don't think this is over, Lumpy!"

Jerry turned his head and mumbled under his breath. "Stuck-up little..."

Tabby shot him a quick look-to-kill that stopped him in his tracks.

He sighed, and decided that it might be more advantageous to get the conversation back on track. "So, where do we go from here?" Jerry asked as he got up and readjusted his robe that he had been using to cover himself up.

Glimpin thought for a moment. "We need to avoid the servant for now. Let's concentrate on finding the Caster first. He and Jerry's scroll can't be too far away. Doubt he'd be in the phone book being a teacher, we'll have to get his information at the high school."

"You want us to break into the high school and steal faculty records?" April asked. "Now this might be fun!"

An all too familiar ring tone erupted from the cell phone next to a figure hiding out in the corner of a dimly lit room. He picked up the phone and quickly pushed the answer button.

"What is it?"

"Everything is going to plan. The kids and the freak are heading to the school to find out more information. Should I call the cops and have them stalled?"

"No. I rather enjoy the cat and mouse hunt. Keep with them and report what they find to me. Are they on the right path?"

"They are close, but they are barking up the wrong tree."

"Good, Glimpin will regret getting involved with trying to stop me again. This time I will make him pay for his meddling, and he still has no idea who he is up against."

The figure ended the phone call and leaned back into the corner of the room. A smirk crossed his face. "Soon my master, after all these years, we will have our power, and our revenge."

Chapter 9

As the veil of deception lifted further from Tabby's eyes, the more she could see things were drastically changing around her. Houses and trees were leaning as though the ground had become wrinkled. Sidewalks were twisted and sunk into the ground. The cars on the side of the road which looked nice yesterday were becoming dented and rusted.

What is going on here? She thought to herself as she and the others walked to the high school. *This place looks as though it were hit by a bomb, or an earthquake.*

"If you think it's bad now, just wait, it gets worse," Glimpin said looking up at her knowing exactly what she was thinking about.

"How can no one see all of this? How could they possibly not see how run down and decrepit our little town is? What about people from outside of town, don't they see it?"

"To be truthful, this is what much of the world looks like. People are blinded by their arrogance. They believe that everything is rose peddles and daffodils, but in truth, it is all weeds," Glimpin answered as they continued to walk. "One day people will see, and that is when things will really change. You can't take from nature and not expect repercussions."

"Why is the root of the mystic tree hiding the truth?" Tabby asked.

"It doesn't really. It only personifies one's perception of the world. Let me ask you this, do you think warthogs are beautiful?"

"Umm...no, not even a little."

"But to another African warthog, they are." Glimpin said.

"I see, I think."

"So if the root completely dies..."

"Then the veil is lifted on everyone. The real world would be revealed to them. The world would go into a panic, fingers would get pointed, riots would erupt, and governments would collapse, chaos would ensue..."

"And people would be vulnerable to a new world power who could put things right, the power of the Caster," Tabby finished.

Glimpin stopped for a moment, looked up at Tabby, and smiled. "You know, for a kid, you're pretty smart. I'm just sorry you had to get involved in this mess," He started to walk again. "I wasn't going to tell you the truth. I was going to throw you and your friends out. I didn't want you to be in danger. I've been around for hundreds of years looking over and protecting the root."

"Glimpin, I'm really not much of a people person. I hold what few friends I do have very close," Tabby said as she put a hand on Glimpin's shoulder. "No one should have to face all this by themselves. No matter how capable you are. I'm not going anywhere now. I may not like everyone at my school, or much of anyone for that matter, but I can't just sit by while someone out there is trying to destroy it."

"Thanks, I just hope we are able to find the Caster before your boyfriend there is stuck that way forever," Glimpin replied with a huge smile on his face.

"AAAHHH! Not you to!" Tabby yelled. "I told you all that the walking, talking, arrogant, superficial, self-centered, fragrantly overwhelming car freshener is not my boyfriend!"

April jumped in, "Sounds more like your trying to convince yourself of all that rather than making a judgmental observation."

"Did I miss something?" Jerry asked looking dumbfounded.

"Nothing dear," April answered, "Nothing at all."

The night air surrounding the high school was cool and stale. The moon light was snuffed out by the clouds that were moving gently from the west. A layer of mist just barely visible to the eye had welcomed to group as they approached the school.

The main entrance of the school looked more like a mausoleum than a portal of education. The tall pillars which flanked each side of the door seemed to glare down upon the uninvited trespassers.

Tabby felt nervous as she approached the locked doors of the school. Something in the air just didn't seem right. She felt like they were being watched.

"Is anyone else getting the feeling that something is not right about this place?" Tabby spoke out as they stood on front of the double doors.

"Nope," answered April. "Nothing weird about two girls, a hunchback creature, a mythical gnome, and a vampire dog getting ready to break into the local high school looking for the last known address of an evil wizard bent on ruling the world."

"Thank you, Miss Obvious", Tabby replied smartly as she took the small piece of wood Glimpin had given her out of her coat pocket and waved it in front of the door. The lock clicked and the door swung open.

"Hey! I need to get me one of those," April said as she started to walk into the school. "Do you think that thing works on diaries too? My older sister must have all kinds of cool things written in hers."

The four walked through the front door and looked down the corridor. The hallways were darkened and eerie. What little light that did trickle in from the outside cast ominous shadows down the hallway walls. The floor was lightly littered with a bit of debris which danced around in the light breeze to some unknown melody.

"Are you sure we will find what we are looking for here?" Jerry asked as they peered down the hallway.

Tabby turned to Jerry, "Well, if you think about it, if they need him to come in and substitute, they have to call him, which means they have to have his number written down here somewhere. Let's try the office first."

"We need to hurry," April added. "I'm sure that someone is bound to notice we are here."

"Agreed," Glimpin added, "let's get a move on."

Outside of the high school entrance stood a tall lanky figure wearing dark colored pants, a dark colored hoody with the hood up. He stared intently into the school entrance. A dark and sinister grin began to form across the figures face. "Now I have you Glimpin Dimbwick, right where I want you."

From inside his hoody pocket he pulled out a small piece of paper and a pencil, scratched something down quickly, and then slowly began to walk to the entrance.

There is no place left to hide.

Chapter 10

"Whoever hired the secretary here needs to sack her. Nothing here is in any sort of reasonable order," April observed as she filed through a tall stack of papers that were piled up on top of the desk. "She makes Glimpy over here look like a neat freak."

"How could tackling her make her a more organized secretary?" asked Jerry with a puzzled look on his face.

April gave Jerry a blank stare. "Are you really that dense?"

"Not as dense as that eye make-up," Jerry shot back with a grin on his face.

"Well isn't that strange?" Tabby broke in before the sparks could start flying. "I am looking at this year's detention records and there doesn't seem to be any record of you being here last Friday."

"Really, I may not be the brightest star in the sky, but I'm positive I was here. Maybe they haven't entered the information," Jerry remarked.

"I would have thought so, but this week's detention records are already logged in after you would have been here."

"You think that's strange?" April added. "Our estranged substitute teacher was relieved of teaching just two days before you bumped into him in the hallway. It says here he was observed as being intoxicated and acting erratically towards fellow teachers."

"Sounds like your lackluster theories are beginning to turn into cold hard evidence Tabby," Glimpin said as he reached up and removed his hat. "Do we have an address on this guy?"

Suddenly a loud resounding voice roared from down the hallway as the foursome turned quickly in unison to see what was coming. "I've got you now Glimpin Dimbwick! You won't get away from me!"

All of a sudden, from out from the darkness came the tall lanky frame of Simon. He was panting either from excitement, or running all over the school trying to find them. He stopped just short of the doorway leading into the office, stared horrifically at Jerry, and dropped to his knees. "Oh no, not you again, please don't kill me!"

Simon crouched down to the floor and assumed a sort of fetal position.

Jerry walked over and yanked the quivering heap off the ground and stood him up. "Why are you following us?"

"I…I…I just wanted to see Mr. Dimbwick with my own eyes. I…I'm his biggest fan," Simon managed to get out. Then he looked over at Glimpin and his eyes began to widen. "Oh my god, you…you…you're a forest gnome! This is awesome!"

"How do you know what I am?" Glimpin asked.

Simon shrugged out of Jerry's grip and took a few steps forward. "Well for one, your oversized nose curves closer to the bridge of the nose which is slightly different than your garden variety gnome. Second, your ears point more forward than a rock gnome. It's all in the observation."

Glimpin looked blankly at Simon for a moment. "Really, and none of the fact that I'm standing right in front of you and real is not bothering you one bit?"

"Oh no, I've believed in this kind of stuff since I was little, I'm just excited that now I can go back to my Castle & Orcs gaming group and tell them I was-"

"No!" The group yelled in unison.

"Oh I get it," Simon replied to the group's insistence. "This is a 'covert' operation. Ok, I can keep it under wraps. So, what are we looking for?"

"We?" April asked as she looked him down like an uninvited guest at an all-girls slumber party. "Jerry, kill him."

"Wait!" Simon shouted with a horrified look on his face as he shot Jerry a quick glance then back to Tabby. "Look, sweetheart, I'm smart on these things, I can help, please?"

Tabby looked over to Glimpin who was still a little stunned about the sudden intrusion. He thought for a moment, then reluctantly sighed and nodded his head. Jerry, who at this point had a hard grip of Simon's shirt, equally reluctantly let go.

"I'm watching you," Jerry warned.

"Cool, so who wants to fill me in on the adventure so far?" Simon asked as he pulled out a small piece of paper and prepared to take notes.

"Well," Tabby started to explain. "We are looking for an address for a certain substitute teacher from the high school that was fired last week."

"You're referring of course to Mr. Emit Spader right?" Simon asked.

"Um, yes," April answered quickly. "And how exactly did you know about that?"

"I'm a journalist, sort of. It's my job to know everything," Simon answered back just as quick. "It was on page twelve of Wednesdays afternoon's addition of the paper, line ten. He lives at 1313 Salem's Flame."

Glimpin tilted his head to one side. "I think I'm going to like this guy."

"Never mind that now! How in god's green and blue earth could you possibly know that?" April asked insistently.

"Well, I've never told anyone this before, but, I somehow have the ability to remember and recall anything I read, and where I read it. It's a curse," Simon admitted.

"Still a lot better than my curse," Jerry replied. "At least you can still walk around in public without starting a panicky riot."

"You mean you're under a curse that makes you look like that? I wonder if it has anything to do with The Scrolls of Corum?" Simon wondered out loud.

"That's what we're thinking," Glimpin replied.

"HOLD ON!" April screamed as she threw both arms up in the air in a stopping motion. "Does anyone else think this geek knows way more than he should?"

"Relax, sweetheart," Simon said in a nonchalant tone of voice. "It's all documented in the Castle and Orcs game chronicles first edition collector's series from 1981. Who do you think wrote it? He's standing right here."

Tabby turned to Glimpin with a shocked look on her face. "So, you told the whole world?"

"Hey!" Glimpin shot back, "Like I said before, the best place to hide something, even secrets, is sometimes right in front of people's noses."

"So, Simon, you can see everything going on around here that others can't?" Tabby asked.

"See what?" Simon replied as he looked around him, "Nope, everything seems normal to me."

"Not even the half crumbled wall behind you?"

Simon turned and stared at the wall for a few moments, then looked back at Tabby as though she were crazy. "You must need a new pair of glasses, my love."

Tabby could see Jerry's fist tighten from the corner of her eye. She ignored it and looked at Simon as though she was going to strangle him. "Can we please just stick with the first name basis before I beat you to a bloody pulp?"

"Sure thing, sweetie," Simon replied. "So you think Spader is our Caster?"

"We're pretty sure at this point," Glimpin answered. "Do you know where this house is?"

"Yep," Simon replied.

"Good," Tabby said as she turned around and started to walk out the door. "Let's get out of here before someone sees us or I strangle Simon to within an inch of his life."

"I'd prefer the latter myself," Jerry added as he walked past Simon and the others.

"What's his problem?" Simon asked Glimpin as they followed the others out the door.

"Who knows?" Glimpin answered. "I could never follow the logic of teenage love."

"I heard that!" Tabby screamed from the end of the hallway.

Tabby and Jerry walked in silence several yards ahead of the rest of the pack. She was pondering to herself why Jerry tightened his fist back at the high school when Simon called her 'my love'.

Was he getting angry because he thought Simon was being an unwanted flirt and that I was taking offence to it, there by going into defense mode for me, or... was he jealous? She wondered.

She looked over at Jerry as they walked. He was very quiet, looking at the ground as he walked. The look on his face seemed like something was troubling him.

Maybe he's just getting edgy about the countdown to when he would look like a hunchback for the rest of his life. I guess that would make anyone edgy, She reassured herself and turned to look to see where she was walking. She could hear Simon, April, and Glimpin talking amongst themselves just behind them. They were carrying on about exactly how they were going to stop Mr. Spader from trying to rule the world. Surprising to even her, up to that point since they had left the high school, she hadn't even thought about what they were going to do as soon as they found him. She thought to herself that she needed to focus if she was going to save the world, and Jerry.

Something, indeed, was bothering Jerry. His head was simmering with the thought of turning around and knocking Simon into the middle of next week. It swirled around in his head so much that he nearly forgot the task at hand.

Why am I so concerned about him? He thought to himself. *I know he's not a threat to us or Tabby, but why am I so angry with him?*

He turned his head and saw Tabby turning her head away and look down to the sidewalk. He couldn't help but notice how the light evening breeze blew one of her pigtails across the side of her face and back against her neck. He quickly turned away and looked back down to the sidewalk himself.

Maybe it's just me, but I never really looked at her before, He thought to himself again. *She's winy, anti-social, overbearing, unstylish, temperamental, weird, not to mention just plain to look at. There is absolutely nothing about her at all that really stands out, and yet, for some odd reason or another, I can't help but notice her. Is there something wrong with me, or is she all of a sudden becoming...important to me? Or maybe the more appropriate word would be...special?*

Chapter 11

The five-some arrived about three or four houses from Mr. Spader's house. They all looked at each other bewildered as to what their next move was. After a quick moment or two, Glimpin decided to take the reins.

"Ok, April and Simon, you two head to the back of the house and see if you can find him. Me and Tabby will head towards the front. Jerry, get on top of the house and check the windows, and whatever you all do, don't be seen."

"Right," everybody said in unison and began to part in their separate ways. It was clear that April was not at all happy with the arrangement, but for the time, was remaining quiet.

Glimpin and Tabby walked slowly up to the front of the house. Their luck was holding out, there were bushes lining the front of the house, and they could stay relatively hidden. They both crept up to the first window and peeked in.

The place was a disaster. The entire floor was littered with newspapers and envelopes. Half eaten food covered a good part of the dining room table, which looked as though it had seen better days. The walls were partly ripped out exposing the insulation and electrical wiring. Parts of the ceiling were torn out as well with the chandelier hanging precariously by a few electrical wires. The carpet, barely visible from the garbage that covered it was ripped to shreds as well. Chairs were turned over and other furnishings broken and turned over as well.

"Wow," Glimpin observed as he peered around what must have been the dining room. "And I thought I was messy."

"You're not messy, you're lazy." Tabby replied as she looked around the room as well. "A problem I plan to fix as soon as we finish this little adventure. But I will admit, you have nothing on this guy. He must have killed the maid."

"You aren't kidding. This place would be The Federal Emergency Management Agency's worst nightmare," Glimpin added as they continued to search for any sign of life. "If I didn't know better, I'd say there was some kind of struggle, or someone or something broke in."

"Well, let's get in there and get that scroll," Tabby insisted. "We're only wasting time sitting here staring."

Glimpin looked at Tabby cautiously. "You're right, let's get in there. But we need to be careful. Something about this doesn't seem right."

Simon and April walked quickly around the back of the house. All the lights on this side of the house were darkened except the light in the basement. The two moved closer to the window, it was steamed up and impossible to see through, but the two could definitely make out some kind of movement.

"Do you think that's him?" Simon whispered as the two bumped heads trying to look in the window.

April gave him a quick shove away from her. "First, don't get fresh, second, who the heck else would be in here?"

"So, what do we do?" Simon asked as he recomposed himself.

"We go in, that's what," April answered as she stood up and began to creep up to the back door.

"Are you crazy? Glimpin didn't say anything about going in. Do you even realize what we're up against in there? This is probably one of the most powerful wizards in the world. He could turn us into toads with a blink of an eye."

"That is exactly why you're going in first, lover boy," April explained as she took a step back, grabbed Simon's shirt and half dragged him to the door.

"Why should I go first? This is your stupid plan," Simon protested quietly as they approached the door.

"Several obvious reasons. One, you're a man. Two, I'm a woman. And three, if you get a jump on this 'wizard' before he can conjure up this toad spell, you'd be the hero."

Simon thought to himself for a moment. "You are right of course, besides, I know about this kind of stuff. Just one thing before I risk life and limb marching into the back of the domain of a diabolically evil wizard bent on world domination?"

"What?" April asked.

"Can I have a kiss?" he answered as he puckered up his lips like a strange, ugly looking fish.

It didn't take Jerry long to reach the top of the house. Everything looked quiet from where he was at. He took a few moments to check the windows when he noticed one was partly open.

Well, guess it couldn't hurt to climb in here, check everything out and let the others in. Jerry thought to himself as he slid the window quietly open and made his way to the inside.

The inside of the room was dark. Jerry couldn't make out anything in the room. An unsteady feeling blew through him like a gust of wind as he fought to adjust his eyes to the darkness. After several seconds, a dark figure appeared on the other side of the room. It was clothed in a long black tunic, its face completely darkened from view.

"Well, Master Jerry, I am impressed by you and your friends ability to find the right path quickly. I will have to be more vigilant in any future undertaking."

"Are you this Caster everyone is talking about?" Jerry asked as he took a step forward to get a better look.

I wouldn't come any closer if I were you. I am not without my defenses after all. Nor am I unaware that your friends and the freak are already inside the house, and in very real danger."

Jerry stopped in his tracks. "What do you want?"

"What do I want?" The dark figure asked with a chuckle. "The more important question is what do you want?"

The figure tossed a book out of the darkness which Jerry quickly caught. He looked down and saw it was a high school year book that had his picture on the front. A picture of what he used to look like.

"You see Master Jerry, your only desire is to be normal again, back to your handsome self. My only desire is to throw the entire world into chaos and terror only to rebuild it again in my master's image, and with me as its ruler. Seems simple right? Well, there is this little thing getting in my way-"

"The root of the mystic tree." Jerry finished.

"Exactly!" the dark figure continued. "You see, I have to drain the power of the root in order to bring forth the power I need to rule over all."

"But the root is already dying, why do you need me?" Jerry asked.

"Oh, that root would never die or run out of energy on its own. That is why I need to drain it of its power using the scrolls."

"You didn't answer the question, why me?"

"Now that is a good question. Let's just say that it is not draining fast enough. I need someone that has great influence over the youth of your forsaken high school to fool them into signing the scrolls and becoming part of my minions. If I'm able to cover all the scrolls at once, the power drain would be complete and this pathetic world would finally see that which was hidden from them. They will see what wretches they really are and cities and nations will crumble. I will become their savior and become all powerful!"

"What makes you think I would help you?" Jerry asked as he clinched his fist and threw the yearbook off to one side.

"Another good question indeed, well, you tell me how this sounds?" The dark figure replied as it started to make its way towards Jerry. "All you have to do is sign this little piece of paper making you my servant forever. I'll give you your dashing good looks back and you convince your little friends at school to do the same, simple enough."

"And if I refuse?" Jerry asked as he began to inch his way back to the window.

"Then you all will die in this house tonight, starting with that little girlfriend of yours. And if you were lucky enough to escape with your life, by tomorrow night, you will remain a hideous beast of a man for the rest of your miserable existence," the figure said with a fierce menace in his voice.

Tabby! He thought to himself as he backed into the window. *No!*

"Well, sir, what is your answer?"

Jerry thought for a brief moment. "If I do this, I would never be able to forgive myself. Nor would Glimpin, April... Tabby..."

"Well?!" The dark figure insisted as it drew even closer.

"NEVER!!!" Jerry screamed as he threw himself forward at the dark figure in front of him.

The figure instantly turned into a cloud of dark mist as Jerry tried to make contact. He could hear the figure speak through the mist as it disappeared. "Very well then."

Glimpin and Tabby about jumped out of their skin when they ran into Simon and April in the living room next to the kitchen. After catching her breath she asked, "You guys see anything?"

"The only thing we saw was some movement downstairs in the basement. We were getting ready to head down there," Simon said as he was catching his own breath and rubbing what looked to be a seriously red hand print on his right cheek.

"We better take it easy going down there," Glimpin said as he made his was around the group pulling a short dagger out of his coat sleeve. "If something goes wrong, get out and forget about me, I will be Ok."

"NEVER!!!" They could hear Jerry's voice ring out from upstairs.

"It's Jerry!" Tabby screamed. "He's in trouble!"

All of a sudden the floor beneath their feet started to rumble, followed quickly by a defining noise as though a thousand wolves were howling at the moon at once. It nearly shook everyone off their feet.

"I think we're all about to be in trouble!" Glimpin warned as he turned to the others.

Suddenly the floor near the front door shattered into a million pieces as a horrible four-legged monster erupted from the basement below and clawed its way onto the first floor. Its back was reared like a pit bull ready to strike. Its fangs were at least three inches long and had a tail like a serpent. It growled fiercely at the group as it took a quick moment to bat at one of its ears, as though it itched, then its eyes began to burn a bright burning crimson and orange.

"What the heck is that thing?" Tabby screamed as she and the rest of the group began to backup slowly.

Glimpin grabbed Tabby's and April's arms and quickly pulled them down to the floor. "HELLHOUND!" he screamed. "DUCK!"

The rest of the group barely hit the floor as the beast all of a sudden burst into an inferno of flames and shot a ball of fire out of its mouth, just missing them by inches over their heads. Glimpin began to push the group into the kitchen just behind them. "Hurry, we got about thirty seconds before it reloads, if it doesn't rip us apart first."

Everyone began to quickly file into the kitchen except for Tabby who was looking towards the stairs leading to the second floor. "Jerry!" she screamed as the Hellhound began to lurch forward towards Tabby.

The room around her was quickly catching fire. The floor, walls, and ceiling were lit up. Suddenly another crash, and from the ceiling Tabby saw Jerry fall through the floor and land right on top of the Hellhound just as it was about to snap it's jaws at Tabby's face. Jerry wrapped his arms around the beast's neck and pulled its head up and away from her as she turned to get up and escape the flames.

"Get out of here! I'll hold it off!" Jerry yelled as he continued to wrestle with the beast.

"I'm not leaving y-"

"GO!" Jerry yelled again as he pulled up again on the neck of the beast as another ball of fire spewed from its mouth and struck the ceiling just above Tabby's head.

She ducked her head as she was expecting the ceiling to come down on her when she felt a hand grab her from behind and yank her into the kitchen area before the ceiling could come down on her. She continued to kick and scream as the unknown hand continued to drag her through the kitchen and out the back door to safety. She continued to scream for Jerry as the unknown rescuer dragged her closer and held her.

"I thought I was going to lose you forever!" a familiar voice rang out, it was Thomas.

Tabby started to cry as she watched the house begin to collapse in flames. "No, Jerry!" She buried her face into Thomas's chest. She couldn't watch as the rest of the house went down in flames. From a distance, she could hear the sirens scream of the fire department.

"We need to move before the firemen get here," Glimpin said. "Before they see us and start asking questions."

"I can't leave without Jerry," Tabby said with tears running down her cheek.

"You don't have too," another familiar voice said.

Tabby looked up and saw Jerry crouched down beside her and Thomas. He had a look of relief on his face. His cloths were tattered and burned, still smoking from the flames. Tabby let go of Thomas and grabbed Jerry and hugged him tight. "Don't you ever do that again!"

"No promises," he replied as he looked up at Thomas who was looking a bit abandoned. "Thanks for getting her out of there in time. I wish I had a friend as dedicated as you."

"You do, my friend." Thomas replied as he put a hand on Jerry's shoulder. "Now, you do."

Chapter 12

The five teens sat in a circle back at the news building while Glimpin rifled through mounds of old books feverishly. April had been very silent since they left, which was very unlike her. Thomas, Tabby and Jerry were talking about what their next move should be. All four agreed that they needed to verify that the Hellhound was dead then go after Zack to see if they could get any information out of him regarding the Caster's whereabouts. Simon was in "La-La Land" as he looked around the room at all the old books and newspapers. He was holding Fang on his lap petting him behind the ears.

"It's kind of late don't you think?" Glimpin asked as he turned briefly from his pile of books. "I'm sure your parents are going to start worrying about you."

"April's mom thinks we are at my house," Tabby explained.

"Tabby's mom thinks we are at my house," April added.

"Parents are out of town" Thomas jumped in.

"Haven't been home in two days, parents don't care," Jerry said.

"I'm seventeen and gifted, I'll do what I want," Simon finished as he looked over and made a flirtatious eye gestures towards April. She turned her head and made a puking sound.

"Did you find anything out on how we are supposed to fight or kill a Hellhound yet?" Tabby asked as she turned to face him.

Glimpin looked up from the book again, "YOU, are going to do nothing of the sort. You guys are in enough danger as it is. I will take care of the Hellhound, you guys will concentrate on finding this Zack guy and see if he tries to make contact with the Caster."

April stood up and looked at Glimpin, "Really, do you really think that you are going to be able to defeat a 300 plus pound beast by yourself! You're barely 4 feet tall, you're barely a quarter of his size. We will need to work together on this, so what is our move?"

"I'm not so sure we are dealing with an actual Hellhound anyways," Tabby added as she brought a finger up to her temple and began to tap. This was Tabby's classic thinking pose.

"What do you mean?" Jerry asked.

Tabby stood up and began to pace the floor. "Something was weird about that Hellhound."

April looked at Tabby with a stupid look. "Um, it was a Hellhound, that's not weird enough for you?"

"It's not that. When the Hellhound jumped through the floor, it stopped to scratch its ear." Tabby recalled as she stopped pacing and looked up at April. "Oh...my...god! That thing had to be-"

"Mr. Spader?" Jerry finished.

"Glimpin, you said the Caster can't be the artist, and the artist can't be the Caster. Does that also mean the Caster can't cast on himself?" Tabby asked as her eyes began to widen.

"No," Glimpin replied. "The Caster can't cast upon himself."

"If you're right," Thomas jumped up. "Then Mr. Spader cannot be the Caster."

"This means we are back to square one trying to find out who the Caster is." April added as she threw herself back down on the floor and buried her head in her hands.

"Maybe Zack is the Caster?" Jerry assumed as he began to stand up.

"That's silly," April answered. "I think Zack is just a little too young to have figured out how to use that kind of power."

"I have to agree with her." Glimpin said as he turned away from the pile of books. "We can't just assume that the Hellhound was this Spader guy, we need more proof."

Tabby began to look very unhappy. "I'm almost certain it was him, what kind of a howling, ravenous beast stops to scratch its ear before attacking someone? Think about this for a moment."

"I do not doubt you Tabby, but we have nothing to go on but a hunch." Glimpin replied. "But right now, we have a sacked substitute teacher, an over-zealous second string quarterback, and a dangerous spell caster bent on world domination to find. Let's start with the kid."

"Fine, I got a few choice words for him anyways, let's move!" Tabby replied back as she turned to head out the door.

Jerry's head quickly jerked up. "I get it now! Sacked means fired, right?"

"I think we need to stop for a little while and try and take a quick nap before we continue," April shot out. "It's like midnight, no use being half asleep trying to find Zack, Just for a couple of hours or so."

"It might not be such a bad idea," Thomas seconded the motion, "Let's just stop for a moment."

"Jerry has less than twenty-four hours before he is stuck this way forever, and you want to sleep?!" Tabby yelled.

"It's OK," Jerry reassured her, "I'm feeling a little run down as well. Maybe an hour or two to clear our heads wouldn't be such a bad idea."

"Fine!" Tabby replied with a little regret in her voice. "Only a few hours though. It should give Glimpin some time to figure out how we can fight this Hellhound anyways."

"I'll do my best," Glimpin said as he turned to look at the mounds of books in front of him. "Simon?"

"Yes?"

"Can you give me a hand here? Two pairs of eyes are probably better than one," Glimpin asked.

"No problem!" Simon answered as he stood up and walked over to Glimpin's side at the table.

"You know he won't forget anything he reads in those books of yours, right?" April asked.

"Doesn't really matter at this point, does it?" Glimpin replied as the two turned and got to work. "Guess he's one of us now."

The first hour seemed like an eternity to Tabby as she sat on the floor next to the front door of the office space. She found it difficult to sleep and gave up. She was on her MP3 player listening to music. Jerry was equally finding it hard to sleep and decided to crawl over and sit down next to Tabby. He leaned over to hear what she was listening to. Tabby gave him a quick nudge as to say he was getting too close.

What is he doing? She thought to herself as she began to notice that her heart was doing that irregular beat thing again.

"What are you listening to?" he asked.

"Somehow I doubt that you would like music that isn't driven by modern commercialism or popular social stereotyping." Tabby snapped. "This is true artistic expression from the heart, not for a paycheck."

Jerry thought for I second, "I don't think I quite understand everything you just said, but try me."

"Ok then, Jasmine Rodgers."

"Who the heck is that?" Jerry responded as he tried once again to get close enough to hear only to be cut off yet again.

"She is only one of the greatest musicians to come out of the UK," she replied. "Do you want to listen to what real music sounds like? Or would you rather me try to download some of that regurgitated popular junk they play at the local hit station?"

"Sure," he replied with one eyebrow raised. "I'll give it a whirl."

She removed one of the ear buds and handed it to Jerry who placed it close to his ear and listened for a few minutes.

"You know, she's no DJ RoughHouse or Dr Sideous, but it is nice in its own way. She has a lovely voice," he observed as he continued to listen. "It's like comfort food for your ears."

"It is." Tabby replied as she pulled the ear bud out of his hand and placed it back in her ear. She turned sideways slightly and stared away as though she was trying to ignore him, which she was.

"Are you trying to push me away? Are you nervous about something?" Jerry asked with a sharp tone to his voice. "One minute you act like you care, the next, you're trying to ignore me. What is the deal with you?"

"Let's just call it, self-preservation of one's personal feelings." Tabby replied with an equally sharp tone.

"Look, I get it!" he tried to explain. "I was a jerk. I figured out one day a few years ago that I was good at sports and people thought I was dreamy for some reason. I let it go to my head and deserted everyone who had been my friend up to that point in my life in exchange for popularity among the masses. I did it for selfish reasons, but I never truly intended to hurt anyone by it, especially you."

Tabby turned and faced him. "Really, and in less than a day, you will have your trim body, your good looks, and your old friends back exactly the way it was before, then what?"

Jerry started to say something when Tabby intervened. "I'll tell you what will happen. You'll go back to saying nothing to any of us lower life forms while you return to your normal routine of goofing off, butting heads with the jocks, and having a scent detectible by 300 yards. Nothing will change with you."

"If you really believed that, then why are you helping me?"

"Because unlike you, I don't turn my back on my friends!"

"How do you know I can't change?"

"Cause you're no better than the rest of the cattle!" she yelled, then noticed that everyone was staring.

"Fine!" Jerry said as he stood up. "I'm sorry for inconveniencing you!"

He turned and darted out the door without another word. Everyone started to stare at Tabby. She felt a little uncomfortable.

Thomas walked over and kneeled down next to her. He could start to see the tear come out of her eye. "Look, I think you were being just a little harsh there. He can't help who he is. But you don't make his or your situation better by shutting him out. He's making an attempt to-"

"I don't care! I will not let him hurt me again," she interrupted.

Thomas looked at her for a moment. Then his face changed to despair. "I knew it. You're falling for him aren't you?"

"No! I don't like him in the least little bit like that. He's my friend...and that's all it can ever be...he...couldn't..." Tabby could not get the words out.

"I think you should just leave her alone kid." Glimpin said as he put a hand on Thomas's shoulder. "Someone go get Jerry and tell him we found a way to fight the Hellhound, we leave now."

"Just one last thing Tabby," Thomas said before he turned to go out after Jerry. "I think that you're amazing and beautiful, I wouldn't doubt it if at some point, if he hasn't already, that he starts to see it too. Now, stop being a jerk to him and let him prove himself."

Tabby looked down to the floor and wiped her eyes dry. "Go get that lug and let's finish this."

Chapter 13

"He gone!" Thomas shouted as the group bolted out the door.

April glanced around quickly. "Where do you think he went?"

"I hope he didn't try and go face that beast himself, that thing will rip him limb from limb. He got lucky the first time. I doubt that thing will let him get away again," Glimpin replied as he finished stuffing a few supplies into his bag.

"Of course he will try. He doesn't want us involved anymore." Thomas said as he turned and looked at Tabby. "But the only lead we got left to figuring out who the Caster is-"

"Is Zack," Tabby finished as she turned and started down the alley way.

"Where are you going? You don't even know where this guy lives," April screamed as she and the others started out after her.

"He rides on our bus. We get picked up third on the route, so that will put him somewhere in the Wilted Estates area," Tabby explained as she turned the corner and was stopped in her tracks.

"Well aren't we ob...serv...ant," April was able to get out before an extremely bright light shot at her face.

It was the guard from the front lobby. He had been out patrolling the outer perimeter of the news building and now was staring down three minors who were out well past curfew. A strange smile and look of accomplishment appeared on his face as he leaned over to get a better look.

"Well," The guard asked, "What do we have here?"

"We were just on our way home," Thomas replied as they attempted to move around the guard who quickly cut them off.

"I don't think so!" he shouted. "First you're trespassing on private property. Second, you're a minor and out after curfew which is against the law. And third…"

"They are with me," Simon said as he quickly turned the corner and maneuvered around to the front of the group.

"Really, are you their parent or legal guardian?" he asked.

"Umm…no," He replied as he took a quick look back at the clan and nodded in Glimpin. "But their uncle is right around the corner."

Glimpin hurried and threw on his hat and walked around the corner where the guard could see him. "Is there a problem, Bob?"

"Are you Glimpin Dimbwick?" The guard looked on with a hint of excitement in his voice.

Glimpin placed a hand in his pocket and smiled graciously. "Why yes, yes I am."

Bob quickly lowered his flashlight and breathed a sigh of relief. "Thank God! I have wanted to meet you for some time now Mr. Dimbwick."

Glimpin dug his hands deeper into his pocket and continued to smile. "Really, why?"

"To kill you of course!" Bob screamed as he reached over to his belt and began tugging on something which for some reason wouldn't come out.

"Everyone get down!" Thomas yelled as he grabbed Tabby and April and pulled them back away from Bob who was still yanking away at his belt.

"Your knife has a wooden handle. I thought your master would have taught you better than that?" Glimpin replied as he pulled a wicked looking dagger out of his pocket and began to rush at Bob.

He bashed Bob in the belly with the pommel of his dagger and waited a brief moment as Bob began to fall down to his knees from the blow, then turned around and held the dagger to his throat. "OK now, who is the Caster and where do we find him?"

Bob began to laugh whole heartedly as he leaned back slightly and looked over at Glimpin with an evil looking smile. "Really, you think you're going to get an answer out of me? Obviously I'm not the only one who didn't learn much from their masters. Go ahead, slit my throat. I'm not telling you anything."

"As you wi-" Glimpin replied as he began to swipe the blade, but was cut off.

"Wait!" Tabby yelled as she rushed up and grabbed Glimpin's arm. "You can't just kill him, he's a human being."

"This guy is a servant. I've suspected it for a while now. He used to try and follow the pizza guy into my space a few times which is why I keep the door locked," He replied with a sad look on his face. "Once you're a servant, you never go back to normal. Even if the scroll you signed is destroyed, or the Caster is killed. The servant will only continue to carry out his orders to the end. Besides, he's not quite human anymore anyways."

Bob began to struggle a little back to his feet. Glimpin kept a firm grip on his shirt collar and tightened up blade up against his throat. Then, with one precise swipe of the blade along his neck, Bob began to crumble into a pile of dust on the ground.

"I'm sorry dear," Glimpin said as he put a hand on Tabby's shoulder. "I know it must seem harsh and mean, but this is a war, there was no turning back for him. It just shows you how important it is now that you're in the loop, to be careful of everyone, trust no one, and be prepared for the worst. That's why I didn't want you kids involved, but since you are now, you need to be prepared. This is probably not the last of the servants we'll face."

Tabby looked down at the pile of dust on the ground and back up at Glimpin. "How did he go from being a human being to a pile of dust? Are the scrolls responsible for that too?"

"No," Glimpin answered as he held up the dagger. "This is the Earth Blade. A mystical weapon forged from the flames of Mystical Tree. There are four such weapons in existence. Each one holds the power of a different element: earth, fire, water, and air. The other three have been lost for some time now."

"At least he didn't suffer Tabby," April said as she got up off the ground from where Thomas had practically tackled her.

"Yea," Tabby answered as she looked back down at the pile of dust that was slowly starting to blow away in the night breeze. The only thing remaining was his cloths and belt. Tabby leaned down and grabbed the knife from Bob's belt and his wallet. She opened the wallet and dragged out a bunch of cards and some papers.

After a brief moment of inspecting the contents of the wallet, Tabby handed April his driver's license. "Go to his apartment and see if you can dig anything up there. Take Simon and Thomas with you. Me and Glimpin will head towards Wilted Estates and see if we can find Zack before anyone else tries to kill us."

"What makes you think Zack is going to tell you anything? We didn't get anything out of this guy," April asked.

"We have to try," she answered. "Besides Jerry is still missing, my bet is that he's going after Zack himself, which means he's in danger."

She turned to Thomas and handed him the knife. "You heard what Glimpin said, trust no one."

"I'll make sure nothing happens, I promise," Thomas replied as the three headed out.

Please, Tabby thought to herself as she turned and faced Glimpin who was picking up the rest of Bob's belongings and throwing them into the dumpster nearby. *I hope we find Jerry before he does something stupid.*

Glimpin turned from the dumpster and took a few steps forward. As if by some sort of instinct, he seemed to know exactly what and who Tabby's thought were with. "Don't worry, we'll find him."

It didn't take long for the two to get to Wilted Estates. The neighborhood, once surrounded by lush trees and bushes had become what could only be described as a wasteland. Trees were dead and leafless, vines seemed to have completely taken over much of the landscape, the streets were crumbled, and houses looked like they were mostly deserted. To Tabby, the whole scene reminded her of a creepy grave yard.

Tabby suggested to Glimpin that they start on the furthest of the three blocks that made up the estates and make their way back to the front, he agreed. The objective was to look for any evidence of where Zack lived, and then wait it out to see if there was any sign of activity while they waited for the others to catch up.

As they walked down the first street, they could hear the sounds of the night echo through their ears. The crickets seemed to chirp in unison as the two made their way from house to house looking for any signs of life. In the distance, the two could hear faint sounds of talking and laughter. It was the only lead the two had, so they listened and followed the sound of the voices to a small two-story house towards the end of the middle block.

As they approached the house, the laughter got louder and louder as did what sounded like a constant shushing noise as though that knew they were being too loud.

"SShhh...," They heard one of the voices, "If you get too loud you'll wake up my parents, then it's it for the night."

"Awe, poor baby," A female voice said, "Not ready to give me up for the night yet?"

"Not ever," Said the first voice as Tabby could hear kissing soon after followed by the unison of sighs.

Tabby could feel her gag reflex come in as she thought to herself. *God really, get a room you two.*

The female voice spoke up again. "Oh, I've been working on that new poem of mine, want to hear it?"

"Sure, I love to hear your poetry."

Gag! Tabby thought again as she made a puking face at Glimpin who was trying to keep a straight face.

"OK, here it is," the second voice said as she cleared her throat and started. "Upon a stone one night she sat, a lovely corpse in midnight black."

What kind of poetry is that? Tabby thought as she continued.

"The rock below spelled out Denise, and for seven years she'd been deceased."

Suddenly there was a slight sound of stick snapping in half. The boy on the porch suddenly leaned over the edge of the porch and looked directly at the pair hiding just below. "Who's there?"

"Sorry, it's dark and couldn't see where we were...Adam, is that you?" Tabby answered looking somewhat awkward as she slowly stood up from her hiding place, with Glimpin following suit.

"Tabby? Tabby Grimshaw? What are you doing here in this part of town?" Adam asked as he turned to Lisa who was sitting right next to him. "Lisa, you know Tabby from school right?"

"I think I've seen her around before. How are you doing dear?" Lisa replied as she sat up straight and offered a hand. She was wearing the ugliest pink polka dotted pajamas Tabby had ever seen.

Tabby in turn reached out her hand and grabbed hers. "Nice to meet you, I think I've seen you around before to. Aren't you on the cheerleading squad?"

"Yes, yes I am...wait, you're that April's friend aren't you?" Lisa asked nervously.

"Relax, she's off doing something else, nowhere near here," she reassured her.

Lisa sighed in relief. "Thank God, I don't think I could survive another one of her hateful pranks. Some of my skin is still stained from the last one, not to mention the cleaning bill for removing glitter glue from my cheerleading outfit."

"So, you never answered my question. Why are you out this late, and who is your friend?" Adam asked as he leaned back into a comfortable position.

"That is a very good question," Tabby replied as she looked back at Glimpin for an answer and only got a blank stare and a shrug of the shoulders. "Well, this is my uncle...umm...Bob. And as far as being out this late...well...you would never believe me."

Adam stared at her with an inquisitive look and slowly raised one eye brow. "Try me."

Tabby took a deep breath. "Well...OK...umm-"

"Me and Adam spent the better part of a week liberating about half a dozen corpses while trying to vanquish an evil demon from hell," Lisa spoke up as Adam turned and looked at her in disbelief that she told them that. He then slowly turned back to Tabby expecting either a storm of laughter or a recommendation for some sort of therapy or rehab. Instead his gaze was met by excitement and enthusiasm.

"Thank God I thought we were the only ones battling otherworldly forces of evil." Tabby replied. "That was you two, I read about it in the paper."

"Paper?" Adam asked.

"Yes, The Eerie Truth Weekly, you know the local tabloid paper?"

"Oh yea, I know the one. I don't read it though, I just use it to line my cats litter box," Adam replied. A look of anger instantly crossed Glimpin's face. Without looking, Tabby reached back and touched his shoulder before he could flip his lid."

"Well, I wouldn't mention that again, this uncle of mine is actually the writer and editor of that paper," Tabby admitted.

Adam's face turned slightly pale as he looked around to see Glimpin and his less than enthusiastic expression and quickly apologized.

"We are attempting to help a fellow student restore his normal appearance while investigating the whereabouts and identity of an evil magic user called the Caster and stop him from turning the world upside-down and eventually rule over it," Tabby explained.

Adam's face quickly returned to the previous inquisitive mode. "Does it have anything to do with the sudden change in our once surreal landscape around town here?"

"Bingo!" Tabby answered.

"Well I'd come help you save the world, but I'm a little laid up," He commented as he slightly lifted his leg to reveal a cast. "Took some damage at my own escapade, but if you need anything, let me know."

"Do you know where Zack McClure lives?" Glimpin asked trying to move the conversation along.

"Zack?" Adam confirmed, "Yea, next block over, 2011 Closed Casket Lane."

"Thanks," Tabby said as she turned to walk away.

"Wait," Adam said before she could walk off.

"Yes?"

"Wait here a minute..." Adam attempted to stand but was pushed back down by Lisa. She crept into the front door, and after a minute or two snuck back out with a rolled up towel. "This might come in handy."

"How's a towel going to come in handy?" Glimpin asked. "Is it going to rain?"

Lisa shot him a look then unrolled the towel to reveal a dagger that looked strangely similar to the one Glimpin was carrying in his pocket.

"We got it from Hoodoo, you know, that weird Voodoo guy who has that shop downtown next to the funeral home?" Lisa asked as she handed it to Tabby handle first.

Glimpin looked on with wonder. "It's the Infernal Blade. I thought all but mine were lost? I'm going to knock that Hoodoo out. He said he'd never seen any of these things the last time I was in his shop."

Tabby turned and attempted to hand the dagger to Glimpin, who quickly stepped away. "Oh no, only one can handle each blade at a time. I'll explain later."

"It has some great power, be careful with it," Adam said as Glimpin and Tabby turned and walked away.

"Do you think they will be OK?" Lisa asked as she turned to Adam to cuddle some more.

"I hope so."

Chapter 14

April, Thomas, and Simon bickered back and forth the entire way to the small apartment complex where the former servant had resided. Thomas and Simon debated quietly for a moment on who was going to enter his apartment first. Both felt it would be rude to enter while April reassured them that he was dead and probably at this point could care less who entered his apartment.

As they approached the door of the apartment, Thomas double checked to make sure it was the right place. He nodded to Simon as he took a long deep breath and knocked at the door. There was a long moment of silence as the three waited to hear for any activity within the apartment. After what seemed to be an eternity, Thomas gave the door another, louder series of knocks. The three waited once again as once again there was nothing but silence from behind the door.

After another brief moment Simon attempted to knock again when April knocked his hand out of the way and grabbed the keys from Thomas. "Honestly guys, you're acting like a couple of scaredy-cats," she hissed as she fumbled for a moment with the key chain and began to unlock the door.

"Careful," Thomas said as he prevented her from opening the door too quickly. "There could be another Hellhound in there. It could be another trap like at Mr. Spader's house."

"Relax," April countered as she slowly began to open the door and look inside. "Doubt anyone could hide something that big in such a small place."

"True," Simon replied as he followed April into the apartment, followed by Thomas who was shaking he was so nervous.

The inside of the apartment was completely opposite from the house they had previously encountered. The place was completely immaculate. Books and magazines were stacked perfectly on the bookshelf next to the door, mostly war novels and gun magazines. Furniture was placed efficiently around the small living space. There were no dishes in the sink, the bed was made military style, and the bathroom shined. The trio began to look about the rooms looking for any kind of clues.

"This guy must have a lot of time to clean," April observed as she began looking around the bedroom drawers. "Man! Even his cloths are perfectly folded and organized by color. Talk about an organization freak."

"You wouldn't know it by how sloppy the guy looked," replied Thomas as he began rummaging through the kitchen looking for anything out of place.

Simon added as he looked in the hallway closet. "He's obviously hiding any incriminating evidence in the very last spot we would think to look."

"Or," Thomas replied with an inquisitive voice, "right out where everyone can see it."

"What do you...," April began to ask as she followed Thomas' gaze up to the living room wall were mounted perfectly was a dagger that looked incredibly similar to the one Glimpin used earlier. "Is that what I think it is?"

Simon quickly pulled the dagger off the mounting and investigated the handle carefully. "There is no doubt that this must be the Tsunami Blade. I read about this blade in my game, it can control water."

"There's something taped to the mounting behind where the knife was," April observed as she reached up and grabbed a small piece of paper from the mounting and unfolded it.

She looked at the paper for a short time and handed it to Thomas. "There's nothing on it but a couple of names."

Thomas looked at the paper for a brief moment, and then a look of terror began to cross his face. "What was Zack's last name again?"

"McClure, why?"

Thomas stuffed the paper into his pocket and began to rush to the door. "We have to go now, and find Tabby and Glimpin before they find Zack's house."

"Why, what's the problem?" Simon asked as he started out the door after Thomas.

"They are in grave danger."

Glimpin and Tabby made their way around the block and quickly located the house they were looking for. Tabby quickly looked at her watch, 3:30 am. The lights in the house were all darkened, and there was no sign of movement. The two were extremely tired and, after a quick observation of the area, noticed a small shed in the back of the house. The two decided to hold up there till morning and then attempt to approach the house.

As they entered the shed, Glimpin quickly closed the shed door and sat quietly on the floor.

"Guess this is as safe a spot as any," Glimpin observed as he looked over at Tabby who was looking like the walking dead. "You really should try and close your eyes for a while. I don't sleep, so I'll keep watch."

She pulled out the dagger Lisa had handed her a short time ago. "So if I cut someone with this blade, they will turn into fire?"

"No, that's not exactly how the daggers work," Glimpin explained. "They instill the bearer with complete control over whatever element they possess. Only the Earth Blade can transform other objects into dust."

"So how do I control fire with this thing?" she asked as she began to slump over a small pile of garden hoses.

"First you have to concentrate on what you want to have happen, and then the dagger follows the command."

"Who made these things?"

"Corum. It was the other reason he was looking for the Mystic Tree. The power the daggers possess when combined into one can help the Caster harness the evil power that is currently dormant. But only the Caster can combine them. If anyone else were to try and possess more than one sword, the elements of both would overpower the bearer and destroy them. It's for that reason that the blades need to remain separate at all times."

"I see," Tabby whispered as she unwillingly began to fall to sleep.

"Wake up! We need to get a move on," Glimpin said quietly as Tabby slowly opened her eyes.

"What time is it?" she asked as she rose and stretched out her arms.

"About 8:30 or so," he replied as he crept over to the door and peered out into the morning light. "I thought I saw something moving inside the house, someone must be up."

"Oh my god, I completely forgot about the others. What if they were looking for us?" she said as she shot up to her feet and hit her head on a rafter of the shed. "Ouch!"

"SSSHHHH!" Glimpin hissed as he turned to her. "Relax. I've been watching all night, no one has been anywhere near here."

"I hope they're OK," she replied as she approached the door and attempted to look out to see what Glimpin was looking at.

"I'm sure they're fine," Glimpin reassured her as he slowly opened the shed door and started out towards the front door. "Let's get moving before someone decides to mow the lawn."

Tabby thought quickly and stopped to turn and grab Glimpin's hat. "You may want to put this on before we knock on the door."

"Oops," Glimpin remarked as he grabbed the hat on shoved it on his head, looking around nervously. "That could have been bad."

The two made their way quietly to the front of the house and quickly to the front door. The door looked crooked and heavy. The paint job was long past its prime, faded and cracked with several spots that had already chipped away. They looked at each other for a quick moment then took a deep breath and knocked on the door.

Several seconds went by before there was an answer at the door by a woman in an apron wearing the gaudiest sixties style dress she had ever seen. The woman stared blankly for a short moment before putting on her warmest, brightest smile. "Good morning, how can I help you two dears?"

Tabby looked over to Glimpin for a moment to see if he was going to act suspicious like he had before. After getting no weird responses, Tabby looked back at the lady and copied her smile to the best of her ability. "Hi, we're friends of Zack, from school. We were wondering if he was here or not."

"Oh how exciting!" The lady replied as she began to dry her hands on the apron and opened the door wider. "Friends from school, did you hear that, Sweetums?"

"I sure did Snuckums, why don't you invite them in?" another voice chimed from well within the doorway.

"Oh ticky-tacky, where are my manners? Please, you just come right on in and make yourselves at home!" The lady apologized as she gestured for the two to come in.

"My pleasure," Glimpin replied as he began to walk inside the door with Tabby in tow.

Just inside the front door was the living room of the house. To Tabby, it looked as though the sixties had puked all over the room. The walls were covered by old looking wood paneling and decorated by Cowboy and Indian prints. The retro furniture was nearly immaculate with a classic surf style coffee table that really tied the room together.

"Please," A gentleman sitting on a straight-back chair in the room gestured towards a couch. "Sit a spell and try one of my wife's snicker doodles. They are the cat's meow."

"Would you two like some fresh squeezed lemonade? Just made it," the lady asked as Glimpin and Tabby made their way to the couch and took a seat.

"Love some!" Glimpin replied as he stopped for a moment and took a sniff of the cookies that were sitting on a plate on the coffee table. "They do smell good."

The gentleman chuckled, "Darn tootin they do! Go ahead my friend."

"I think I'm fine, had a big breakfast," Glimpin replied.

"Amen to that!" The man replied as he took a puff of his pipe and exhaled slowly while patting his stomach.

Glimpin adjusted slightly on his seat for a moment. "Your pad is pretty boss."

"Thank you, you know, when you're bringing in the bread like I am, only the best," The man chuckled.

"Oh, I can dig," Glimpin agreed as he chuckled himself.

Tabby was lost in translation for a moment. After I little thought she began to get it as the other two carried on. She looked around the room nervously wondering why Zack hadn't appeared yet.

"So," Tabby chimed in, "not to be a bummer, but is Zack home?"

"Well, change the channel will you?" The man chuckled and sat back tightly against his chair. "Don't sweat it chick-y-poo, he cut out to blow off some steam. He was really eating the grapes off the wallpaper this morning if you know what I mean? He'll be back to home plate soon."

"We kind of need to make tracks," Glimpin remarked as he started to rise out of his seat.

"Don't sweat it, have a drink of that fantastic lemonade, its spiffy!" the gentleman replied as he leaned forward slightly.

Glimpin had that look back in his eyes again. "Sure, as soon as you explain to me why there is rat poison in the drinks."

"Well shoot, I was really looking forward to watching your slow and painful deaths," the man replied as he hit a button and stood up.

Just then the front door burst open. Thomas rushed in and looked at the two with a look of terror on his face. "It's a trap, these two are servants too!"

The door suddenly crashed shut behind them and the sound of several clicks from inside the door indicated that it was not going to be the way out.

"Gosh darn it darling, I told you the poison was going to be too obvious!" The lady turned and looked at her husband.

"That's right pumpkin cheeks, you did," the man replied as he walked calmly around to the back of the chair. "So, now what are we ever to do?"

"I guess we do this the old fashioned way," the lady answered as she reached behind her apron and pulled out a machete. "And to think I just finished cleaning up the blood off the rug from the guy that was here last night."

Tabby's heart sank to the bottom of her stomach. *Oh no, they killed Jerry!* She panicked as she reached into her pocket and pulled out her dagger.

"So the hunchbacked kid was here already huh?" Glimpin asked as he in turn pulled out his dagger and moved the couch out slightly to use as cover.

"Well, he was," answered the lady as she worked her way around the room to her husband's side. "But our little ankle-biter wouldn't let us finish the job, insisted that the master needed him for something and dragged him off to the tomb. Not that it matters that you know, because you aren't getting out of here alive."

Glimpin crept slowly over to Thomas who was standing at the door. At this point Tabby had joined him with the lock stick in hand waving it in front of the door.

"Oh yea, that little stick of yours won't work, there is no wood in that door or frame," The man explained, "and your daggers are useless as well. So stop being party poopers and die with some dignity."

"How did you know they were servants?" Glimpin asked Thomas as he tried the lock on the door.

"I think I found a scroll, it had their names on it," Thomas answered as he pulled the paper out of his pocket and handed it to Glimpin.

"Perfect!" he replied as he snatched the paper from his hands. "You two keep them busy, and don't get killed, or cut!"

"You're kidding right? What happened to keeping us out of harm's way?" Tabby asked as she heard the lady in the background raise her machete up in the air and scream as she began to dart across the room to the three.

"Do you really want me to take time to-" Glimpin started as he turned and noticed that Tabby was no longer there and running up to cut the lady off.

Tabby ran up quickly as the lady approached and barely avoided the wild swing of the machete. Tabby fell to the floor and quickly rolled to the right to avoid another possible blow. She quickly stood and darted towards the gentleman who was just getting his own machete and going after Thomas.

Whatever Glimpin has up his sleeve, he better make it quick! Tabby thought to herself as she turned to stand her ground, holding up her dagger and ready to fight.

The lady turned and looked Tabby up and down. "I have no idea what he sees in you, you're ugly and you dress like a homeless person. Who could ever want you?"

Her words stabbed deeper than that machete ever could, and probably hurt worse. She paused for a moment as she began to recall what Thomas had told her earlier.

I think that you're amazing and beautiful... she thought to herself as she held up her blade, her anger started to swell inside her as she began to lunge forward.

Her blade clashed loudly as it struck the machete, sending the lady quickly to the floor. "I'm not perfect, but at least I'm not sporting crow's feet and spider veins!" she yelled as she raised her blade once more for another strike, this time sending the machete flying out of the lady's hands and onto the floor several feet out of reach.

"I need their blood!" Glimpin yelled as rose from behind the couch and gestured at the two.

Tabby turned and poked her blade into the outstretched arm of the lady. She let out hateful scream as the blade dipped slightly into her skin, just enough to draw a little blood.

Tabby then stood up and took a step forward to kick the machete further away and turned to run back to Glimpin who was already standing with Thomas helping him with his battle.

"I got it!" Tabby yelled as Glimpin snuck in beside the gentleman and quickly slashed at his arm and obtaining the other sample.

Glimpin then quickly stepped back and smeared the sample along the face of the paper he held and turned to Tabby. "Quickly, smear it on this!"

Tabby reached forward with her blade and smeared the last sample onto the paper just as she could hear the lady behind her make another battle cry. She turned sharply around to find the lady, with machete in hand lunging toward her. Suddenly, the lady's skin began to glow like a glow stick, brighter and brighter until Tabby could no longer make out her shape.

Then almost as quickly as the glow started, it stopped, and the lady was gone. The machete in midair simply fell to the floor harmlessly. From behind her she could hear the other weapon hit the floor as well.

"Quickly!" Glimpin insisted as he kneeled down on all fours and began looking around feverishly. "Find them before they escape!"

"Find what exactly?" Thomas asked dropping to the floor and mimicking Glimpin actions.

Glimpin didn't answer at first then reached under the table with both hands and pulled out two very unhappy looking gerbils who were thrashing about violently. "Find me something to put these in!"

After a quick search of the house, Thomas was able to find an unused bird cage in the hallway closet which Glimpin quickly stuffed the two gerbils into and sealed the cage door tight.

"That should hold them for now," Glimpin exhaled as he placed the birdcage down on the coffee table and started snooping around the house himself.

"Really?" Tabby asked as she fell to her knees still trying to catch her breath. "Gerbils?"

Glimpin turned and looked at Tabby briefly then turned around to continue his search. "Would you have preferred lions or bears?" he remarked.

"Good point," Tabby answered back as she forced herself to her feet and joined Glimpin. "What are we looking for anyways?"

"Your boyfriend's scroll," He answered as he continued to skim through drawers and shelves.

Thomas looked around the room with a puzzled look on his face. Tabby noticed the strange look and walked over to him. "What's wrong?"

"Does it seem odd that Zack's parents wouldn't have at least one picture of their kid hanging somewhere?" Thomas observed as he walked around the room.

"It does," Glimpin replied as he stood up and began to scan the area himself. "Seems very odd indeed."

"Maybe they're in another room?" Tabby suggested as she scanned the floor and noticed a frame knocked over on the floor.

"All these other pictures have only the parents in them, most of them older photos," Thomas said as he picked up a few of the photos he could find. "Who doesn't have pictures of their kids?"

"Found one!" Tabby answered as she picked up the frame from the floor and examined it. She quickly turned it around and showed it to the other two.

Glimpin's face in a matter of seconds went from curious, to horrified as he slowly walked forward and took the picture from Tabby's hand.

"This can't be," He mumbled to himself softly.

"What is it, what's wrong?" Tabby asked as Glimpin turned slowly and held the picture in the light.

"This can't be! No, no, no, this is impossible! How...?" He yelled as he continued to stare deeply into the picture.

"Glimpin, what's wrong?" Tabby asked in desperation as she grabbed the gnome and forced him around. His face was as white as a ghost.

"Tell me!" she insisted as she knelt down and looked him in the eyes.

"That's Corum."

Chapter 15

Glimpin paced the floor nervously as he mumbled to himself how the wizard could still be alive. Then, as he did repeatedly for what must have been an eternity since the group left Zack's house, rushed back to the huge stacks of books on his desk looking for an answer.

"This is impossible, that man is dead, how is he still alive?" he repeated again for about the hundredth time.

"He's an evil wizard. Maybe he cast a spell on himself to stay young forever?" Simon suggested as he sat precariously on top of a stack of old newspapers.

"Obviously," Tabby answered, "You haven't been paying attention. The Caster can't cast upon himself."

"Oh yea, I remember now. Maybe another Caster cast the spell on him," he replied as he assumed his thinking posture.

"Highly unlikely," Glimpin responded as he walked away from the books again and paced the floor once more. "There is no such spell to make you immortal."

"What doesn't make even more sense," Tabby added, "Is that if Zack is indeed this Corum guy from hundreds of years ago, why would he tell two of his servants that 'the master' needed Jerry."

Glimpin stopped in his tracks and pointed at Tabby with a questionable look on his face. "Your right, that lady did say something to that effect, but I can't put a finger on it."

"Does it really matter right now?" Thomas chimed in, "The important thing is that they have Jerry, and we need to find them quick, his time is running out."

"I agree," Tabby added and turned to Glimpin. "Do you know where this tomb they were talking about is?"

"No," Glimpin replied as he lowered his head and turned back to the books. "There is no mention about any tombs in this area. But I can't imagine they could have gone far."

April finally chimed in as she turned from the small bird cage that now housed two very irritable gerbils. "So, who in this little town of ours would know more about where weird tombs in this area are besides our adorable homicidal gerbils bent on chopping us to pieces?"

Glimpin thought hard for a moment, tapping his finger on his temple, then quickly grabbed his cloak and hat. "Tabby... Thomas...you two come with me. April, you stay here and help Simon put together our little defense against that canine blowtorch, he knows what to do and what he needs."

The three walked quickly out the back door of the news building and started down the alley way.

"So, where are we heading to?" Thomas asked as he struggled a little to keep up with the other two.

"The only person in town that knows everything about this town, a low down dirty voodoo doctor named Hoodoo."

Tabby had passed Hoodoo's Voodoo Shop maybe a million times in her life, and like just about everyone else in the town, never once even gave it a second thought to walk in. The front of the shop, mostly display window with the shades pulled down tight, gave no hint to what may be inside. The slightly narrower than normal door that led inside had what was the only clue that there was anything inside at all, a small piece of ripped up paper about the size of a business card taped to the door with the words "enter here" written on it. The writing of course was nearly illegible and could have been finger painted on by an ant. Beside the small paper sign was what may have been at one time a severed chicken leg, tied to a bit of string, and hanging from the top of the door frame.

Glimpin looked on with a look of disgust. It was apparent to the other two, judging from the look on his face, that this was the last place on earth he wanted to be. He shook his head for a quick moment than turned and looked at the two teens that clearly awaiting his next move. "Don't touch anything! You will regret it."

He then reached up and turned the knob opening the door and quickly ushered the other two in before quickly closing the door behind him. "Hoodoo!" He yelled loudly as the door clicked. "Get out here. I got a bone to pick with you!"

The inside of the shop was a sight to behold indeed. The walls were plastered with all kinds of assorted voodoo trinkets. Candles of just about every scent you could think of to cure ailments and attract/repel evil spirits, assorted styles and sizes of voodoo dolls, skulls mounted on walking sticks with tassels and beads hanging from the bottom of the skulls, rows and rows of old and moldy mason jars filled with assorted herbs and animal parts, and a practically endless assortment of voodoo inspired necklaces. The shelves were practically stuffed to the point where they looked like they were going to collapse. Other unknown objects hung from the ceiling to the point where one had a hard time even making out a ceiling at all.

As Tabby and Thomas slowly made their way to the back of the store with Glimpin, they noticed an old mechanical fortune teller machine that sat next to the sales counter which was also cluttered with a variety of smaller sized knickknacks. Just beyond the counter was a doorway completely covered with a beaded curtain with smoke spewing from the top of an opening.

"I know you can hear me you quack, get out here now!" Glimpin called out again.

"There be no Hoodoo here mon, be gone wit y'!" a voice yelled from the other side of the curtain.

"Yea, and who else would reside in this retched establishment?" Glimpin replied as he approached the counter. "I got what you asked for before."

Suddenly the curtain flew open and an old bald-headed man quickly passed through the opening. "Glimpin! Me ole friend! How bout y'?"

Glimpin turned and nudged Tabby on the arm, "Works every time."

"Be tu long, wa y' want tu pay me fo today?" Hoodoo asked as he put his hands on his chins and placed both elbow on the counter causing several items for fall to the floor.

Glimpin pulled a small bag out of his satchel and began to toss it from one hand to another.

"Ahhh," Hoodoo looked at the bag and chuckled for a moment. "Y' seek knowledge beyond y'. Wa dat y' seeks?"

"A tomb located somewhere near here, probably hidden."

Hoodoo began to laugh hysterically, "Mon, dere be no tombs in these pats..."

Suddenly, and without warning the fortune teller inside the machine moved and a small card popped out the bottom. Tabby, who was the closes to the old machine, reached over and pulled the card out. After a quick glance and a strange look, she looked up at Glimpin and held up the card with the words *'He's Lying'* printed on it.

"Really?" Glimpin asked as he turned again to face Hoodoo. "Stella's not going to let you out of this one today, huh?"

"Steela, mind y' self for me shake y' gears," Hoodoo replied with a nervous look on his face.

Tabby stared at the machine with amazement. "Did that thing just talk to us?"

Another rumble from Stella revealed yet another card which simply said *'Yes'*.

"This is amazing!" Thomas said excitedly as he started to put a hand on the old machine before his arm was quickly snatched up and pulled away.

"You're as bad as a kid in a toy store!" Glimpin said sternly as he looked Thomas in the eyes, then pointed up to the sign hanging on top of the counter which read **'TOUCH IT, YOU BOUGHT IT, MONEY... OR LIMBS!'**

"Oh," Thomas replied understandably and quickly thrust his hands into his pants pockets. "Sorry."

Glimpin turned his attention back to Hoodoo and asked again, "Now, here is the tomb and who is buried there?"

Hoodoo looked a little pale, then looked around and leaned forward. "Is Corum dat be laid ta rest dere," he replied. "Y' no want ta be dere."

Glimpin looked over at the machine which stood silent, then continued. "Corum was cremated at the time of his death and spread along Deadman's Lake, how is he buried in a tomb?"

"Y' be readin ta many books mon, y' connot believe all."

"Are you trying to tell me the ancient achieves are wrong?" Glimpin said with a slight edge of anger in his voice.

"No, bot no complete mon."

"What do you mean not complete?"
"Wa y' seek be amitted."
"Omitted?"
"Das wa I say."
"So…where is the tomb?"
"Y' no say please."

Glimpin stood there for a moment and just stared at Hoodoo with a look that could have blown the whole back of the building apart. He was definitely not amused by his joke.

"Ok, mon!" Hoodoo finally said as he turned and stormed into the room behind the beaded curtain.

Tabby and Thomas could hear the awful sounds of boxes being thrown around vigorously. Stella suddenly moved slightly around within the large black case and spat out another card. It read *'Don't mind him, he's just old and cranky'*.

"Y' no see cranky yt womon!" Hoodoo hollered from the back room as even more boxes started crashing around, spilling part way through the curtain.

He finally emerged with a look of unsatisfied achievement as he slammed an unmarked box onto the counter, knocking yet more small items off.

Glimpin looked on for a few moments in bewilderment. "So…what is it?"

"Da tomb be near da lake, wav dis over da water an tomb will be shown ta y'" he explained. "Na where be me pa'ment?"

Glimpin grabbed the box, and tossed the bag on the counter. "Keep da change mon."

Hoodoo quickly snatched up the bag and inspected the contents carefully. "Pleasure mon," he replied as he quickly turned and darted back to the back room.

Glimpin then turned and faced Stella for a quick moment. "Stella, you are looking as lovely as ever, have a nice day."

Stella bumped around for a short time again as a card popped out. *'Please take me with you!'*. Glimpin laughed and turned towards the door. "Let's get moving, we need to go find that tomb and fast."

Thomas and Tabby started towards the front door and almost in unison, turned back for a moment. "It was a pleasure to meet you!" Tabby said as they turned back around and sprang out the door after Glimpin.

Hoodoo slowly poked his face out from behind the curtain. "Tay go?"

Stella whined for a moment.

"I know dear, tay be in danger."

Outside the shop, Tabby and Thomas caught up with Glimpin, who was continuously lowering the bill of his hat each time someone passed him. He had a look of determination on his face.

"What was in that bag anyways?" Thomas asked as he maneuvered himself to Glimpin's side and tried to keep pace.

"Pieces of my beard hair," Glimpin chuckled with a smile on his face. "For some reason he thinks it keeps his skin smooth and silky."

"Does it?" Tabby asked as she stayed on pace with the other two from behind.

"Beats me," Glimpin shrugged. "Just so long as he keeps believing it."

CHAPTER 16

Almost an hour or so went by before Glimpin, Thomas, and Tabby returned to the newspaper building to complete their preparations for the possible encounter with Corum and/or the Hellhound. Simon, with the help of Sketchy, had all but finished putting together a few backpacks filled to capacity with water balloons. April appeared to be on supervisor duty sitting comfortably towards the back of the room. The gerbils were attempting to rock their cage off the side of a small table just beside her.

"Is everything ready?" Glimpin asked as he walked in from the hallway and placed his newly acquired box down on the table.

"Just finished," Simon replied as he turned to April with a disgusted look on his face. "No thanks to some people in here."

April looked up from the newspaper she had been leafing through for a while now. "Hey! I helped a little."

"Never mind that, we don't have long before the evening will be here. Without knowing exactly what time Corum cast that spell on Jerry, we need to treat every minute like it was the last," Glimpin said as he reached down and grabbed one of the balloons in his hand. "This has to work."

Tabby gave Glimpin a puzzled look as she flipped her attention from him, to the water balloon, and back to him again. "Really, you, Thomas, and Simon mash your brains together for nearly two hours this morning looking for the perfect weapon to fight a three hundred plus pound snarling beast of immeasurable strength, and all you can come up with is a bunch of water balloons?"

"We did find a section of my book pertaining to Hellhounds. It just said they don't like water," Simon replied as he picked up his bag and gave Glimpin a ready to go nod.

"Let's move!" Glimpin suggested as the group exited.

It was around 2 pm as the group finally made it to Dead Man's Lake. It wasn't the official name of the small body of water just west of town though. It really never had an official name. The locals gave it the name back in the 1800's shortly after a series of unexplained drowning had started driving people away. A few selected patrons still frequented the area from time to time, but for the most part the lake was mostly deserted.

Glimpin advised the rest to stay a few yards back as he approached the lake carrying the box that Hoodoo had given them.

"I have no idea what this thing is going to do. Just stay out of the way while I try and figure this thing out," he explained.

The others did exactly as they were told as Glimpin set the box down and opened it for the first time. He looked inside for a moment, cocked his head sideways, then reached in and pulled out what looked like an old, ripped up shoe. He stared at the shoe precariously for a brief moment, then shrugged his shoulders and stood up. He then took another step towards the water and started waving it around.

Everyone couldn't help but giggle quietly to themselves. They all looked at each other in agreement the he looked very silly waving an old shoe out by the water. "I think Hoodoo took you for a ride," April said. "Shouldn't he have given you a magic wand or something?"

"Magic wands are for losers," Glimpin replied as he continued to wave the shoe around. "You've been reading too many wizard novels."

But the amusement was short lived as within a moment or two, the ground below them began to shake. The water in the lake began splash about getting everyone wet. As they fought through the splashing water to see what was going on, they witnessed what looked like a small island rise from the middle of the lake. As it rose further and further from the water, the group discovered that it had a face. They also noticed as the island was rising, the waterline from the shore was receding.

The monstrous face began to turn slowly towards Glimpin, and then came to a rest. The head had to be about a hundred feet tall. No one could imagine how big the rest of this thing could have been. Glimpin bravely held his ground as the face began to smile. "You going to eat that?"

"Huh?" Glimpin replied as he looked around for anything edible. Then he looked back at the shoe for a moment and held it up. "You mean this?"

The giant head began to chuckle. It shook the ground that formed more waves before it spoke again. "No you idiot, the box."

Glimpin looked down at the box, then back at the shoe. "Umm…my friend told me to wave this over the water, you're kidding right?"

"Did your friend tell you to wave that stinky shoe over the water, or did he hand you the box and tell you to wave this over the water?" the head replied with its own question.

Glimpin thought for a short moment, "Ok, you got a point there," He then cleared his throat. "No, good sir, I am not going to eat this box. Would you like to eat it?"

The head began to chuckle again, "What, do you think I'm some sort of sicko or something? Eating boxes, my god, what do you take me for?"

"Look sir," Tabby broke into the conversation feeling that the joke was going to take way too long. "We are looking for a tomb somewhere near here. Do you know where we can find it?"

"Find it?" The head repeated as it turned its attention to her. "My dear, you have found it."

Tabby looked around for a moment then looked back at the head. "Is this another joke? I don't see anything."

"Really, look again," the head replied as it started to move towards the shoreline.

As it approached the shoreline, his head got taller and taller, and more water crept away from the shore. Just as the head looked like it was near the shoreline, the water stopped receding, and its body was revealed. From shoulders to ground, he was about three feet tall and missing one shoe.

Tabby looked again where the lake used to be, and about a hundred feet or so out from where the shore used to be, there was a sealed entrance.

Thomas's curiosity got the better of him. "Sir," he began to ask. "May I ask how your head got so big?"

The head turned slightly in Thomas's direction. "You think my heads too big do you? Well sir, maybe the real question here is, is my head too big, or is your head to small?"

"Umm-" Thomas replied as the head began to speak again. "The question I personally would be asking myself here is, is my head big enough for everyone to see the sheer beauty that is me?"

April leaned over and whispered in Tabby's ear. "Guess he needs a big head to hold that inflated ego of his huh?"

The head formed a disgusted on its face. "Like you're one to talk little miss, I can see your nappy slit ends and slowly clogging pores from all the way up here."

April opened her mouth to protest just as Thomas placed a hand on her shoulder and shook his head. She quietly closed her mouth again and crossed her arms tightly in front of her. "He's lucky his nose is so far up there or I would have made it bleed," she whispered.

"How are you holding yourself up?" Thomas asked as he stared in bewilderment.

"Having been blessed with all this perfection and beauty is indeed a chore. It is not easy being perfect," the head spoke as it began to sit down slowly and raise its shoeless foot. "Now would you be so kind as to put my shoe back on for me? As you can see, I have a hard time seeing what I am doing. Beauty is pain you know."

"I see," Simon observed as he took a step forward. "You are using the buoyancy of your head in the water to help relieve the weight from your shoulders."

"Oh you simple minded fool," the head chuckled. "The water keeps my skin moist, radiant, and beautiful. All this sun wreaks havoc on my immaculate complexion"

Glimpin finished putting on the head's newly rediscovered shoe. "OK, it's done. Let's get in there so he can get back in."

"What's the rush?" The head inquired, "What could be even half as important as gazing upon all that is me?"

Not puking in my mouth, Tabby thought to herself as she picked up her backpack that was crammed full of water balloons. *Or, pulling my fingernails out with a pair of pliers.*

"OK…I get it…too much to take in at once, I completely understand," the head said as the group gathered their supplies and started for the tomb entrance. After a few minutes of pulling and tugging, the entrance slid open and the group made their way inside. Glimpin slid the door back shut behind them as they could hear the rush of water begin to refill the lake again.

The corridor just inside of the tomb entrance was too dark to see. Glimpin and Thomas immediately took out their flash lights and inspected the area around them. The dark cave that led downward, deeper into the tomb was lined with moss and dripping water from the lake above. The top of the cave measured about six feet from the floor and was about five feet wide. Both floor and ceiling were covered partly with sharp stalagmites and stalactites. The smell of stagnant water engulfed their nostrils.

April took a brief moment to look back at the entrance that they had just passed through. "Did anyone think ahead as to how we were going to get out of here after we finish whatever it is we are here to do?"

Tabby looked around for a moment, "Well, this place doesn't look as though it's been travelled anytime recently. Perhaps there is another entrance into this place?"

"That would be Hoodoo's style, sneak in the back door and hope to take them by surprise," Glimpin replied as he swallowed hard and began to make his way down the cave.

"You mean we could have skipped having to listen to Mr. Full-of-Himself?" April asked as she half-stumbled just behind the rest of the group.

"Just watch your step and your voice, "Glimpin answered as he continued. "Or I'll leave you here when we're done."

The group walked on for what seemed to be almost an hour before reaching a small chamber where they all agreed to stop and take a rest. As Thomas shined his flashlight around, he began to notice unfamiliar writing on the walls of the chamber. "Does any of this make any sense to you, Glimpin?"

Glimpin looked on with a sudden interest as he slowly ran his hands across the letters then turned around and continued reading from the other side of the wall. "Oh boy."

"What is it?" Tabby asked as she stood up and walked towards the dumbfounded looking gnome. "What does it say?"

"In short, these are the writings of a poor sap that got lost in here, he never found the way out," Glimpin explained as he continued to read on.

"How do you know he never got out?" Simon asked as he leaned back up against the wall, adjusting himself from an uncomfortable lump on the floor.

"Cause your sitting on his head," Glimpin replied as he pointed to the skeletal remains just under him.

Simon jumped up quickly letting out a high pitched yipe as he did so. He turned quickly as he looked in horror at the partly dressed remains. "We're all going to die!"

"Put a sock in it brainiac!" Tabby yelled, "Get a grip, no one is going to die down here. Glimpin, does it say anything about where we are heading or how much farther it is?"

"It's pretty damaged from the water, but I think there is a fork up ahead," Glimpin replied as he squinted his eyes and tried to make out any other words.

The rest of the group started looking around the chamber looking for additional clues as Glimpin stopped reading for a moment and started thinking to himself. He looked over to April who had just begun to settle herself down on a rock in the middle of the room. "WAIT!"

Just as April sat back on the rock, it began to sink into the floor. She quickly jumped to her feet and began to fidget around. "Umm...what was that?"

Just as she had said that, a rumbling sound began to fill the air along with the sound of splashing water from the corridor they had just come from. The water noise was faint, but was beginning to get louder and louder.

"MOVE!" Glimpin yelled as the group turned and began to run down the next corridor on the other side of the room.

About a hundred yards or so they came to a fork in the road which contained yet another set of unknown writings. Glimpin carefully yet quickly read the writing, then threw his hands up in complete frustration. "It's some sort of riddle. I can't make it out!"

As the sound of splashing water got louder and louder, Simon looked at the two separate corridors, one continued in a downward path, the other upwards. "We need to take the high road, or we will drown."

"Hold on!" Tabby said as she turned to Glimpin, who was still trying to make out the writing.

"It's too faint," Glimpin said as he quickly rescanned the writing on the wall. "Something about looking up to see down, or something."

She thought about it for a second, nothing seemed to be out of place to her. She looked around again as the others started arguing with her, telling her to hurry up as they turned to walk up the higher path.

"WAIT!" she yelled as she looked to the ground and noticed there were no stones laying on the ground. She then reached into her pocket and pulled out a penny. She held it out for a moment then gave it a little toss. The penny hung in mid-air for a moment, then shot straight up and stuck to the ceiling. "We go down, hurry!"

"Are you crazy? We'll drown!" April screamed as the rest of the group started looking at each other.

"Down is up!" Tabby screamed as she grabbed April and pushed her through the downward passage.

Glimpin and the rest reluctantly followed as the sound became almost deafening. "I really hope you know what you're doing." Glimpin yelled as he made it out of the fork and partly down the corridor. He turned a few yards up and stopped, "Get up against the wall!"

Just then, a rush of water splashed into the corridor, rolling vigorously along the ceiling and began to spill upwards into the other corridor. Glimpin thought for a second, and then gave Tabby a hard pat on the back. "That was some fast thinking there. Good work."

"What the heck is happening here?" Simon asked as he watched the water splash past them.

"We are on the ceiling, somehow," Tabby explained as she pointed up to the ceiling. As the others followed her finger up, they all began to notice that there were assorted rocks and debris lying above.

"How is this happening?" Thomas asked as he reached up, grabbed a rock and let go, only to watch it fall back onto the ceiling again.

"I don't know, but I'm sure we will probably find more tricks like this as we move along. Speaking of which, we should hurry, who knows when that water is going to catch up with us," Glimpin said as he encouraged the others to continue quickly down the corridor.

"I agree, let's get a move on!" Tabby concurred as they made their way onward.

"Does this mean we are heading upward then?" Thomas asked.

"Yes Thomas, this means we are heading upward," Glimpin replied as they moved along.

"And we are walking on the ceiling?" he asked.

"Yes Thomas, we are walking on the ceiling," Glimpin answered again.

"So, when does gravity take over again?" Simon asked taking over where he thought Thomas was leading to.

"Hopefully soon." Glimpin replied with a hint of annoyance in his voice. "So you two will fall on your heads and stop asking stupid questions."

CHAPTER 17

It seemed like forever as the group continued their way up the passageway. Of course the never ending borage of questions continued throughout the trip. Not to mention April's constant complaining about her feet hurting. The passage narrowed in quite a few spots where the group found themselves squeezing between the walls just to get past.

"May I ask a question?" Tabby inquired as she worked her way to the front of the line with Glimpin.

Glimpin turned his head and looked at Tabby. "What is it?" He was surprised he hadn't heard from her much in the last hour or so.

"What exactly will happen to Jerry if he signs the scroll? Will he just instantly do Corum's bidding, or fall asleep, or become faint?" Tabby asked as they continued.

"Nothing out of the ordinary, but the Caster would have to give an order quickly to make sure the spell is complete. Jerry would not be mindless per say, but he will follow his orders to the tee."

"And there is no turning back huh?" Tabby inquired again.

"Well, there might be one way, but it has never been proven." Glimpin went on to explain. "The Caster himself cannot take the life of another being. If he does, he loses all his power. It could be argued that by losing his power, those under his power would be released, but I can't say for sure."

"So, if Zack...I mean Corum... were to kill someone, then those two gerbils would be restored to normal?" Tabby wondered out loud.

"Look," Glimpin said as he grabbed Tabby's shoulder and turned her around. "Those two are only alive because of you and your reaction when I killed Bob. I, or we for that matter, cannot afford the luxury of trying to spare all of them. I'm pretty sure that Corum/Zack is more than aware of his limitations, and is going to go out of his way to ensure he doesn't kill anyone. That is why he has servants to do his dirty work for him."

Tabby turned her head away, the idea of hurting another soul because of this business made her both upset and mad. "What if Corum already talked Jerry into making him his servant? Are you just going to kill him?"

"Sorry kid," Glimpin replied as he turned and started walking again, "Trust me, I'd be doing him a favor."

After another ten minutes or so, Glimpin turned to the group and told them to shut off their lights. Just as he thought, from ahead of them, there was a faint sign of flickering light.

"We must be getting close, everybody quiet," Glimpin whispered as he motioned for the group to move ahead.

As they inched closer and closer to the light, they began to make out voices that were still indistinguishable. But there was no doubt in Tabby's mind that it was the voice of Zack.

As they finally reached the light, Tabby and Glimpin stuck their head out from around the corner to survey the area. The chamber was huge and circular which towards the top formed a sort of dome. The top of the dome was opened up and the early evening sunlight could be seen shining onto what looked like a makeshift altar.

Kneeling on top of the altar was Jerry, who looked like he'd been beaten pretty badly. His hands were bound behind his back and some sort of collar was placed around his throat. Standing just a few feet away was a dark clothed figure that was pacing the floor in front of a table which contained various vials of unknown assorted fluids and several large pieces of paper. And as they assumed, the Hellhound was circling around the altar, staring Jerry down like a fresh piece of meat.

"You know you're but a short 15 minutes away from looking like that for the rest of your natural life?" the figure spoke as it walked away from the table and approached Jerry. "You may as well give up and sign the scroll."

"Bite me!" Jerry replied as he attempted to spit across at the figure only to miss by a mile.

"You know, my other servants may have already killed those precious friends of yours. They are a bit old fashioned, but are very capable of handling a few little teenagers. Maybe if they are still alive, I'll have them hauled here where you can watch my little pet here chew them to pieces while you watch," the figure threatened.

"Leave them out of it! This is between me and you!" Jerry yelled.

The figure laughed deeply as he took yet another step towards the altar. "Is that what you really think? Guess we will find out soon enough." The figure turned suddenly towards the opening where the group was hiding. "Won't we... Glimpin!"

"So much for a sneak attack," Glimpin said quietly as he straightened himself up and walked cautiously through the opening into the chamber. The others filed in just behind him with water balloons in hand.

"Well, my old friend, welcome to my humble abode," the figure said with his hands and arms stretched out. Then reached up and slid back the hood of his robe to reveal his face. It was indeed Zack.

"I'm no old friend of yours, Corum!" Glimpin snapped back as he pulled his dagger out from his coat pocket and removed his hat. "I could never call a monster like you a friend."

Corum laughed again as he took a few steps forward. "So, you do recognize me, your memory serves you well gnome. Tell me now how many times have you gotten in the way of completing my ultimate objective of ruling over these mindless human masses?"

"Quite a few, but I never imagined it was you I was up against. You've hidden yourself well over the years, and maintained your youth as well. Now will you tell me how you've been able to accomplish that?" Glimpin asked as he started to circle slowly around the room towards the altar.

"That, gnome, is a secret I will take to your grave," Corum replied as he raised a hand, then the Hellhound stopped circling the altar and joined his master at his side.

"What's the matter can't do your own dirty work?" Glimpin asked as he raised his dagger in Corum's direction.

Corum brushed off the remark. "If it were up to me, I would slice you up into a million pieces. But, you know how it is, rules and stuff. Anyways, this could be far more entertaining. How will it end I wonder? Your friend here is about to become a hideous monster, you and your other friends are stuck facing insurmountable odds against a killer beast with nothing more than a dagger and a handful of water balloons. You tell me how it will end, brother."

"Let them go and I will sign!" Jerry yelled finally.

"Well," Corum replied as he turned and looked at Jerry. "That is more like it."

"Wait!" Tabby interrupted as Corum began to walk back to the table. "I will sign if you restore Jerry and let the others go!"

"My dear," Corum stopped and looked at Tabby, "Why would I want you as my slave?"

"You saw me Friday, just a little dress and make-up made half the guys at our school drool all over themselves. I could get your signatures and form your army of slaves in no time," Tabby swallowed hard, "Not to mention having me be whatever you want, and do your every bidding."

"Ah!" Corum replied, "Now you do have my complete attention. You really are a strikingly beautiful young woman when you want to be."

"Don't do it Tabby, this is my problem not yours!" Jerry called out as he began to struggle with the rope that was holding him back. "You lay one finger on her and I will kill you!"

"Oh!" Corum looked over to Jerry then back to Tabby. "Now this is interesting, Looks like your boyfriend objects to your little proposal?"

"He's nothing to me, I just don't want my friends getting hurt, that's all," Tabby replied as she began to step forward. "Where do I sign?"

"Are you nuts!?" Glimpin replied still holding his ground as he held the dagger up towards the Hellhound, "If you sign that scroll, you will be his slave forever! I can't fix this one!"

"Do we have a deal!?" Tabby yelled as she ignored Glimpin's words.

Corum thought for a moment, and then an evil smile formed across his face. "Deal."

Tabby began to walk quickly to the scroll, picked up the old quill pen and began to sign. Tabitha Grimshaw

"NO!" Jerry yelled as he fell to his knees and started to weep.

"I should have spoken up sooner," Glimpin said as he dropped to his knees and dropped his dagger to the ground.

"What do you mean?" Thomas asked as he reached down and touched Glimpin's shoulder.

"Jerry's curse can't be cured. It has to be transferred to someone else," He explained as he dropped his head in defeat. "There is nothing we can do for either one of them now."

Tabby paused for a moment after she signed the scroll. Then looked up from the table and faced Corum who was looking quite pleased. "What will you have me do first my master?" She asked.

"Oh, this is fun!" Corum replied gleefully. "This is so much better than I anticipated. First my dear, kiss me."

Tabby walked over to Corum slowly. Once she had reached him, she slowly wrapped her fingers behind Corum's head and kissed him on the lips. She could hear Jerry struggle more with his rope, then stop.

As she released she looked Corum in the eyes. "Is there anything else my master?"

"As a matter of fact there is my dear," Corum replied as he slowly turned his attention to a weeping Jerry, who looked like he was giving up all hope. "Kill him."

"You two had a deal!" Thomas screamed as he started to take a step forward towards the Caster only to be cut off by the Hellhound, whose eyes began to glow red.

Tabby looked over at Thomas, "Don't you worry lover boy, you'll get yours soon enough I'm sure," she then turned her attention to Jerry. "Should I make it quick and painless, or make him suffer, a lot?"

Corum thought for a moment, "Whatever makes you happy my pet."

An evil grin formed on her face as she pulled out the dagger from her coat pocket and slowly began to walk over to Jerry.

"We need to do something!" Thomas said as he attempted to maneuver around the Hellhound only to be stopped again.

"We're too late, we are no match for the three of them," Simon answered as he dropped his bag and slumped to his knees. "Are you willing to kill Tabby?"

"We have to help her!" Thomas began to cry.

"Nothing will turn her back now, it's done," Glimpin watched in horror as Tabby reached Jerry on the altar.

"Poor, poor little lover boy," Tabby started as she placed her fingers gently on his face and caressed his cheek. "Life is so unfair isn't it? You only now in the very end really show me just how much you care. You do care about me don't you?"

"Yes, very much so."

"Tell me, before I slice your throat, just how much you care about me."

"I...I would do anything for you. The last few days you have been there for me, even if you were being a jerk at times. But I understand now, it's probably the same way I would have treated you if none of this would have happened. But now, I want to be there for you too. I want to be by your side when you need help. I won't give up on you anymore. I... I think I'm fa-,"

Tabby threw her head back and laughed loudly as she moved behind Jerry and began to rub the blade across his face. "I don't think you are even capable of caring about anyone but yourself you little maggot. Do you actually want me to believe that you of all people could have ever cared?"

Corum looked on with great pleasure. He slowly started to rub his hands together.

"I'd hoped I could have made up for my mistakes. Guess it's too late for that, huh?"

"Oh, you're quite right about that," Tabby answered as she moved the blade down to his throat. "But, before you drown in your own blood, would you do me one last teeny-weeny favor lover boy?"

"Whatever will make you happy, Tabby" Jerry said as he closed his eyes expecting the end to come.

All of a sudden he felt the rope come loose from around his wrist and he quickly worked his hands out.

Tabby grabbed the rope that was holding the collar around his neck and pulled back till their eyes met. "Beat the snot out of that second-string loser like you should have the first time!"

She slashed her blade quickly along the rope that held Jerry's collar, cutting it completely in two. Jerry took a quick look at Corum whose expression suddenly turned very grim. "It would be my pleasure!" Jerry answered as he instantly hurled himself at the half suspecting Caster and knocked him off his feet.

"NOW!" Glimpin yelled as he jumped to his feet and began to chase down a very confused Hellhound who quickly lunged out of the way and turned in the confusion awaiting an order.

Jerry was indeed knocking the stuffing out of Corum who turned between blows. "Don't just stand there you idiot, kill the other's now!"

The Hellhound instantly sparked into flames as it turned to Thomas and Simon and started to snarl. The two looked at each other for a quick moment then almost in unison plunged their hands deep into their bags and snatched up the first load of water balloons and held them in a ready to throw position.

"Is it just me, or did this seem like a good idea up to about a second or two ago." Simon observed as the beast began to creep forward towards the pair.

"I'll answer that question later when I can think straight. Right now I'm just trying to keep count and control my bladder," Thomas replied quickly. "28...29...30! RUN!"

The beast bellowed out a fireball as Thomas and Simon split into different directions and let loose the first barrage of water balloons. They both missed as the beast lunged back and begun to run around the outer perimeter of the room in an attempted to pick off Simon first. Thomas counted out loud as the two attempted to regroup before the beast could fire another fireball. Shortly after the two met back together, Glimpin rejoined them as the count reached twenty five.

"Tabby, look for Jerry's scroll!" Glimpin yelled as he grabbed a water balloon and hurled it at the Hellhound, striking it on its side. The beast yelped loudly as the water balloon splashed along it's side, putting out a small portion of its flaming fur, only to reignite quickly.

"Thirty!" Thomas yelled as he ducked down and threw himself out of the way of another fire ball.

Tabby quickly turned her attention to the table containing the pages of papers, and then broke out in a mad dash to reach it before anyone else could. She began grabbing and inspecting the papers quickly, but had no success in finding the scroll containing a picture of Jerry's monstrous form. "It's not here!"

"Keep looking!" Glimpin replied as he ducked under a table and out the other side just as the Hellhound jumped on to the same table then fell through clumsily.

She continued to look around for the scrolls as she witnessed Corum starting to gain a foot in his battle with Jerry. *Where the heck is that thing?* She thought quickly to herself.

Glimpin, Thomas, and Simon continued pelting the beast with water balloons to no avail. Glimpin threw his last balloon as he backed into a wall that the other two had just met up at. The three looked down at their bags and back at the beast that was 20 seconds from turning them into ash. They were cornered.

"Well," Simon said as he crouched down in a fetal position. "Looks like this is the end of us."

Glimpin and Thomas held out their individual daggers in defense. "I'm not going out like this," Thomas said as he looked at Glimpin and nodded. "On three?"

"On three," Glimpin replied as he turned to face the beast for what may be the last time.

"One…two…,"

Suddenly the ground began to tremble, louder and louder. Even the beast seemed to get a little uneasy as it stopped to scratch its ear. Shortly after the rumble started, a faint sound of splashing could be heard from the entrance the group had used to get in.

"Thomas, can you use that dagger?" Glimpin asked as he began to take a few steps away from the entrance.

"I'm a fast learner," Thomas replied as he raised the Tsunami Blade up and waited.

The beast reared up its head, ready to unleash another fireball. Glimpin looked around desperately and found an unbroken water balloon. He quickly picked it up and threw it as hard as he could towards the Hellhound's mouth, a perfect shot. The beast took a couple of steps back as it coughed and choked on the water.

Just then the entrance exploded with a huge wave of water. Thomas closed his eyes and concentrated hard on the dagger in his hands. Suddenly the water began to lift up off the floor, and swirled around the ceiling, faster and faster with each rotation. Then, without any warning, the water shot down like a huge fist right at the Hellhound. The water smashed hard into the side of the beast sending it crashing into the wall of the chamber. The Hellhound then collapsed to the ground.

Thomas was breathing hard as he just stood there motionless for a moment. "D...d...did I just do that?"

Glimpin walked over and patted Thomas on the back. "Good work kid, now go help the others, I've got a hunch about this thing."

"Right!" Thomas replied as he started off to the other side of the room after Tabby and Jerry who were both now trying to take on Corum.

Tabby and Jerry were indeed having a hard time with the Caster. With every swing he would disappear and rematerialize behind them knocking them off their feet. They had almost all but given up on defeating him.

"There has to be a way to stop him from disappearing like this?" Tabby observed as they once again attempted to take a swing only to meet with the same results.

"I remember this!" Simon said as he stumbled up behind her and Jerry. "He can't jump if you can get a grip, and once he jumps he can't change where he materializes"

Tabby gave Simon a quick look then over to Jerry. "As soon as I swing, jump backwards as far as you can."

"I got you!" Jerry replied as he waited for the moment.

Tabby lunged forward again with her blade in hand to take another swipe at Corum. As he started to disappear, Jerry flew backwards as fast as he could. As Tabby predicted, Corum materialized just behind Tabby, and well within Jerry's reach. Jerry reached forward and grabbed Corum's arm with a death grip, then resumed punching Corum in the head with every bit of energy he could muster.

"HA!" Everyone could here Glimpin raving to himself. Tabby turned and saw the gnome hunched over the now unconscious Hellhound, he was picking at his ear with a pair of tweezers.

"What is it, earwax?" April asked, crawling out for the first time from behind the boulder that she told to hide behind throughout the whole battle.

"Even better," Glimpin replied as he plunged the tweezers deep into the beast ear, fished around for a quick moment. Then with one good tug, Glimpin pulled a piece of paper that was rolled up inside. He quickly unrolled the paper, "Got it!"

Glimpin quickly ran to the table and spread out the paper just as Tabby joined him to look at the scroll as well. Glimpin then looked over at Jerry who had spent a better part of the last few moments knocking the stuffing out of the now weakened Caster. "You got any of his blood yet?"

"Plenty on my fist!" Jerry answered as he landed another blow.

Jerry was starting to glow green as he stopped and looked at his loose hand. "What's happening?"

Glimpin looked over in horror. "Hurry kid, the curse is becoming permanent!"

Jerry quickly let go as he turned and started running towards the table, but was stopped by Corum who grabbed him and dragged him down to the floor once again.

"It's too late! You will never see your true face ever again!" Corum laughed as he tightened his grip, preventing Jerry from getting up. Jerry's green glow was getting brighter and brighter. He reached out in desperation to pull himself along the ground to no avail.

Tabby quickly grabbed the scroll and ran across the room towards Jerry. He was so bright, Tabby could no longer see where he was at. The only hope she had to reaching him was to jump and...

Smoke from the glow had reached every corner of the room. Nobody could make out a thing. Everyone stood in complete silence as they slowly started to make their way through the smoke towards where they thought they had seen Tabby last. The silence was eerie as each one looked quietly to the other.

"She must have been too late," Thomas said as he walked closer to where he had last seen Tabby.

"Ah, I'm so sorry guys," Glimpin added as he walked up to Thomas who had stopped to try and spot the others.

"NNNOOO!!!!" A scream pierced through the room in a nearly deafening cry as the smoke began to clear. Laying on the floor just ahead of them they could make out Tabby's silhouette. She was still holding the scroll, and then another silhouette started to form. As the smoke cleared even more, Thomas's eyes were met by a familiar sight, Jerry had returned to normal. His fist, still covered in Corum's blood, planted right in the middle of his cursed drawing.

Still hidden in the smoke, they heard the angry cries from Corum as he thrashed around in complete and utter rage. "I will make you all suffer for this!"

Glimpin looked out into the haze as Corum's new form began to take shape. Jerry's once hideous curse now belonged to him. "Oh, did I forget to mention, you can transfer the curse to someone else, but the time it takes to become permanent does not change."

"Do you mean that Corum will-" Simon started to ask.

"Look like that for the rest of his days," Tabby finished.

The remaining smoke began to lift away as Corum was now visible to all. Indeed every little disfigured detail was now revealed. He stood high upon the makeshift altar with a small handful of scrolls in his hands. The look in his eyes was dark and sinister.

"Personally, I think he looks better." April commented as the rest of the group started to giggle and laugh. "Can I kiss him next?"

"Pathetic fools!" Corum yelled as he threw his hands up and began to disappear once again. "I will stand at the foot of each of your graves for your interference," The evil Caster then completely disappeared, along with the Hellhound.

Everyone breathed a sigh of relief. They all approached Jerry as he stood up from the ground looking at his hands and arms unbelievably. A tear started to fall onto his cheek as he reached up and felt his real face for the first time in almost a week. He then let out a loud laugh as he looked down and carefully inspected the rest of his body. A huge smile was plastered on his face as he looked up at the rest of the group.

"I never thought I would be normal again," he said as everyone took a turn giving him high fives and hugs. "Thank you all!"

Everyone but Tabby, of course, who had walked away and was staring up at the altar where Corum had just stood. Glimpin walked up behind her and put an arm around her waist.

"You ok?" he asked as he looked up at her.

"You can't imagine how scared I was," Tabby said as she looked down in her hands and stared at the scroll she had signed.

"I was going to ask you how you were able to avoid becoming Corum's slave. I saw you sign the scroll and I thought we'd lost you forever," Glimpin asked.

"Yea," Simon asked as he strolled over along with the rest of the group. "How did you pull that off?"

"I wasn't even sure if it was going to work," Tabby began to answer. "Good thing my mother is a bad speller. She spelled my name 'TABITTHA', with two t's in the middle. You said the scroll had to be signed exactly as it was given by my maternal mother."

Glimpin broke out in laughter, "That, my dear, is a stroke of genius!"

"And it saved my life," Jerry said as he approached Tabby. The others turned and looked at each other as they silently turned and walked away to give the two their space.

"You never gave up on me. You never stopped trying. You...um...did that thing and..." Jerry started to stutter through his words.

Tabby turned quickly and looked him in the eye sharply. "Look, I was in character. I was just trying to get your butt out of a sling. If you hadn't taken off, I wouldn't have had to...to..."

"To...what?" Jerry asked.

Tabby crossed her arms and looked down at the floor. "I wouldn't have had to waste my first kiss on him."

Jerry shared her gaze at the floor, "I...I'm sorry I took off. I promise from now on to learn to rely on you when I need it, but you got to promise to do the same."

"Fine," she replied reluctantly. "But just so you know, I didn't mean anything I said back there when you thought I was possessed or something."

"Oh, um, of course not, I was saying things I thought you wanted to hear to," Jerry replied nervously.

"Yea, that was it," Tabby added as the two stood in front of one another.

Jerry then stepped forward and gave Tabby a long hard hug. "I promise, I will never take you for granted again."

"OK," she replied softly as she wrapped her arms around him as well. "I'll trust you again."

As Jerry began to let go, he turned his head slightly and gave Tabby a soft kiss on the cheek. "Before you cut me off back there, I was about to tell you I thought I was fa-"

"Don't!" Tabby stopped him from continuing.

Jerry smiled, "Fair enough."

The two turned and returned to the rest of the group who all agreed this would definitely not be the time to start pushing couples jokes in Tabby's direction.

"So has anyone figured out how we are going to get out of here?" April asked as she looked up at the opening at the top of the dome shaped chamber.

Just as April said that, a figure appeared at the top of the opening. Glimpin squinted his eyes for a moment then began to wave. "Hey Sketchy, throw us down a rope!"

Everyone could hear Fang screeching in the background as well. They all were looking forward to getting back home, and taking a very, very long bath.

Chapter 18

Life resumed as normal at Eerie County High School that next Monday morning. Of course most of the people at her school, not to mention the rest of the town still looked like walking goons, completely unaware of their own imperfections and ghastly horrific deformities which were all but too clear in Tabby's eyes. But she figured it was not going to get any better so she decided she would just have to live with it.

As the day progressed, Tabby began to notice something else that was very different at school, Jerry. He arrived just after the last bus had pulled out of the parking lot. His hair, which usually was immaculately styled with an assortment of hair care products, looked rather out of place. As well his clothing didn't reflect the usual clean cut and stylish arrangement he was most known for. And as a pleasant surprise for once, one couldn't smell him coming as he strolled up and down the hallways.

His demeanor seemed to have changed as well Tabby thought as she secretly spent the day observing his every move. He didn't really buddy up with the same people he had been. He wasn't mean or impolite, but interacted with them more on an acquaintance level rather than the normal loud and obnoxious "best friend" mentality he'd usually displayed. She began to wonder if his week long experience as a hideous beast had somehow changed his outlook on his personal life.

Maybe he can change. She wondered as she built herself up to approach him in the hallway, where everyone could see.

"So how are you feeling today?" she asked as she stopped just short of the locker he was frantically rummaging through.

Jerry momentarily stuck his head out and smiled. "Much better, and you?"

"Let's just say I have been better," she replied as she felt herself feeling a little jittery. "But, I think everything is going to end up just fine. So, are you heading over to the newspaper later after school? Heard the 'G' man has some stuff to talk to us about," she added.

"Yea, he sent fang over yesterday with a note tied to his collar. Guess you got one too then huh?" he asked.

"Yea," she answered. "So…are you going to start coming to the newspaper regularly?"

"Well," he started. "I wasn't going to at first. I'm not very smart and able to sniff out clues like you guys are. But, I think in some sort of way, I may be able to be of some use to you guys. You know, an extra set of hands or something?"

"Cool!" Tabby said excitedly, and then realized she sounded just a little too enthusiastic. "I mean…yea…we could use all the help we can get."

"Oh," he replied as he turned from his locker and looked Tabby in the eyes. "Besides, you're going to need someone reliable to watch or backside…back…I mean…look out for you. You know…if you get into trouble…or something."

"Good!" Tabby said quickly as she turned quickly and started to walk away from what was turning into an awkward moment.

"HEY!" Jerry yelled, "By the way, I went online yesterday and checked out that Jasmine Rodgers, the singer you let me listen to."

Tabby stopped in her tracks. *He remembered? He was actually listening to me?* She turned and did her best to keep her surprised composer buried. "Yes?"

"Well," he continued, "I found out she used to be in a band called Bôa. I downloaded the CD, and I loved it! Thanks for the heads up."

"Um, sure, no problem," Tabby smiled as she turned to walk away.

~~*~~

Later that afternoon, the whole group was sitting impatiently at The Eerie Truth Weekly office waiting while Glimpin, who was rustling around in the back room. He hadn't really said a word from the time they had arrived, he only asked them to take a seat with a very serious look on his face. The room was very, very quiet.

"OK guys, here they are," Glimpin said finally as he emerged from the back room with five small vials in his hands, placing one in front of each person in the room.

"What is this stuff?" April asked as she inspected the greenish fluid inside.

"It's your get out of jail free card," Glimpin answered.

"Um...what are you talking about?" Tabby asked as she turned to Glimpin, but she knew too well what his answer would be.

Glimpin lowered his head for a moment, and then back up at the group. "Look, I put you guys in danger when I should have kept you all out of this mess. I'm sure you all must be regretting it, so this serum will cause you to forget everything you've seen or heard in the last few days. You will be able to go back to life as normal. All you got to do is drink it before you go to bed tonight, you're off the hook."

The group looked down at their vials together. Then Tabby reached out and pushed hers away. "I'm going to finish this, and make sure he never hurts any of my friends again."

Jerry in turn pushed his away as well. "I can't sit back and let what happened to me happen to anyone else, I'm in."

April and Simon both pushed theirs forward as well, not saying anything as they glimpsed at each other then back to Glimpin. Thomas looked hard at his vial with a very serious look on his face. Everyone else in the group started to think he was going to take it when he lifted his head and grinned. "Well, I guess someone has to stay and clean up your guy's messes." Then he pushed his vial away.

Glimpin's smile couldn't get any bigger as he reached over and grabbed one of the vials. "Good, more for me!" He said as he tipped the vial over his mouth and finished off the fluid in one gulp.

"Glimpin! We can't do this without you!" Tabby yelled as she began to jump out of her seat.

"Relax," Glimpin replied as he wiped a bit of the fluid off his beard. "It was just apple juice with some green coloring. You lame-brains think there is a super-secret formula that erases your memory? Gees, you guys read too many wizard novels."

The group broke out in laughter.

The dark disfigured outline of Corum appeared within a darkened room late that evening. His eyes were full of rage.

Before him was his servant who had fallen to its knees as soon as he appeared.

"You have failed me slave!" Corum proclaimed.

"I did exactly as I was told, my master. You said to stay close and monitor their movements, that was all. I could have killed them all-"

"You could do nothing useful!" he screamed. "Your incompetence has not only rendered me unable to walk freely amongst the masses, but have jeopardized my plans to resurrect my lord and master!"

"My apologies master, how shall I serve you?"

"I still have an ace up my sleeve, and now is the time to use it. You may still be of some use to me. You must follow my orders to the tee. Fail me again, and I'll feed you to the Hellhound!"

April slowly raised her head and smiled. "As you wish, my master."

Would you like to see your manuscript become a book?

If you are interested in becoming a PublishAmerica author, please submit your manuscript for possible publication to us at:

mybook@publishamerica.com

You may also mail in your manuscript to:

**PublishAmerica
PO Box 151
Frederick, MD 21705**

www.publishamerica.com

MAY   2014